WAR GIRLS

Theresa Breslin

Melvin Burgess

Berlie Doherty

Anne Fine

Adèle Geras

Mary Hooper

Rowena House

Sally Nicholls

Matt Whyman

ANDERSEN PRESS
LONDON

First published in 2014 by
Andersen Press Limited
20 Vauxhall Bridge Road
London SW1V 2SA
www.andersenpress.co.uk

2 4 6 8 10 9 7 5 3 1

The rights of Theresa Breslin, Matt Whyman, Mary Hooper, Rowena House,
Melvin Burgess, Berlie Doherty, Anne Fine, Adèle Geras and Sally Nicholls
to be identified as the authors of this work has been asserted
by them in accordance with the Copyright, Designs and Patents Act, 1988.

British Library Cataloguing in Publication Data available.

ISBN 978 1 78344 060 3

Printed and bound in Great Britain by CPI Group (UK) Ltd, Croydon CR0 4YY

CONTENTS

Shadow and Light

by Theresa Breslin

This story is for Bridget

Shadow and Light

'Wicked child!'

The governess's screech brought the housemaid running.

'What's the matter?' The maid gave Merle a sympathetic look. 'I'll fetch a dustpan and clear it up, whatever it is.'

'You can fetch the cane from the stand in the hall,' the governess told her. 'It's a beating that's needed this time. I've never met such a wilful girl.'

As the maid hesitated, the governess pointed to the door. 'Go on! Do as I say.'

'You can't beat me.' Merle's lip quivered but she kept her voice steady. 'Only Grandma should do that.'

'Well, she left me in charge and I will do with you as I please. A few strokes of the cane will teach you not to lose your temper in future.'

'*I* haven't lost my temper,' said Merle.

'Do you hear how she said that?' the governess demanded. 'Absolute insolence!'

'She's just a babby,' the maid protested.

'Eight years old is much more than a baby.'

'Yes, but,' the maid lowered her voice, 'with her losing her ma and da so young...'

'Everyone has difficulties in life. It's no excuse for disobedience and wanton destruction.'

The maid glanced round the room. 'What did she break?'

'These!' With a dramatic flourish the governess indicated a scattering of broken crayons on the table in front of the window. 'I arranged her crayons in the glass bowl in the order she was to use them and outlined the exact shape of the trees in the garden that she was required to colour in. And what did she do? She deliberately flouted me, that's what! Instead of following my instructions, she picked up every single crayon and snapped it in two. Then she grabbed some in both hands and scribbled over my drawings on the paper.'

The governess's voice rose higher as she listed the offences. Although her tummy was aching with fear of the beating to come, part of Merle's mind noted the changes taking place in the angry woman's face: the pupils of her eyes dilating, her cheeks mottling with scarlet splotches. Merle glanced at the red crayon and then at the pink and peach ones. She would need three, or maybe four shades to capture those colours.

'Look at her! She's still being insolent!'

The governess was about to reach what Merle called the Point-of-no-Return. Occasionally, if Merle made herself out to be particularly contrite, summoned tears and begged forgiveness, the governess might pardon her. But if she

4

showed no sign of remorse, then slaps were inevitable.

A ray from the setting sun fell upon the glass bowl. The splintered light spilled across the table.

'Oh,' Merle exclaimed, 'a rainbow!'

The maid ran for the cane as the governess exploded in rage.

'She's not even listening to me!'

Merle closed her eyes as the cane came down.

'You're not even listening to me!'

Merle blinked. Her friend's hand on her arm jolted her into the present, where the screech of the seagulls near the quay outside Calais had reminded her of the Awful Governess fifteen years ago.

'Sorry, Grace,' she smiled. 'What were you saying?'

'I was commenting on the young soldiers on the deck below us.'

Merle laughed. 'The Red Cross information booklet for young ladies volunteering to work in battle zones said that ogling soldiers was strictly forbidden.'

'Becoming too friendly with the men is strictly forbidden,' said Grace. 'But I don't recall being told not to *look* at them.' She nodded towards the artist's satchel slung over Merle's shoulder. 'You could make sketches of the more handsome ones.'

'There was an officer on the quayside who took off his cap for a moment to reveal the most amazing golden hair. But I'd rather focus on seeing France again.'

'Perhaps not the best circumstances to return.' Grace squeezed Merle's hand. 'After three years of war the country will be devastated.'

It would be several days before the girls saw how devastated the French countryside had become.

To begin with they were sent to lodge at the Red Cross base in the Hotel Clairmont and were treated to welcome receptions and dinners. It was on one of these occasions that Merle met the officer with the golden hair.

They'd entered a hall thronging with people and approached the bar in search of a glass of lemonade. The waiter ignored the crowds of men and hastened to serve them.

'There's a fine example of women's rights!'

It was a British voice but talking in French, which Merle had learned as a child. Raising her eyes she saw the reflection of the speaker in the long mirror above the bar. She recognized the young officer whose striking hair she'd admired as her ship was docking.

'They want equality, but are willing to use their femininity to be served first although the men here have been queuing without complaint.'

'The young ladies did not ask for preferential treatment.' The officer's companion was a much older Frenchman. 'And who can blame the waiter? These new recruits to our Red Cross are so pretty.'

'Pretty to look at, but pretty frivolous and pretty feeble under fire, I'd imagine,' joked the captain.

'Then you'd imagine incorrectly, sir,' said the Frenchman indignantly. 'I'll excuse you as it's your first tour of duty on active service. You'll soon find out that British Red Cross ladies are valued and respected here.'

Merle didn't hear the officer's response. But it wouldn't matter what it was. Despite his golden hair, she had made up her mind that he was pompous. She didn't mention to Grace what she'd overheard. There was no need to sour her evening and they'd probably never see that particular officer again.

Unfortunately the table plan was such that she and Grace were seated directly opposite him and were forced to introduce themselves.

He was Captain George Taylor with a responsibility for hospital trains. His companion was Michel Vallon, the Director of the Red Cross for the area around Trécourt, the town between Amiens and Albert where the girls' ambulance unit would be based.

'Do tell me, what made you young ladies join the Red Cross?' Michel Vallon asked in perfect English.

'How could any fit person read the casualty lists after the Somme Battle last year and *not* volunteer to do something?' Merle was aware that her reply was waspish.

Grace glanced at her friend and said lightly, 'Truthfully I am glad to be away from boring Britain. And Edinburgh will be so *dreich* with winter coming on I thought it would be warmer in France.'

'Indeed.' Captain Taylor exchanged a look with Michel Vallon as if to say, 'I told you so!' His face was so smug Merle had the impulse to smack it.

'Yes,' Grace went on, oblivious of the tension, 'I was more inclined to knit balaclavas and socks than join an ambulance unit – which might be situated too close to the Front Line for my comfort – but Merle convinced me otherwise.'

'You can both drive motor vehicles?' said the captain.

'Oh, don't sound so surprised,' said Merle tartly. 'We have also learned how to repair the engine and change tyres.'

Grace stared at her.

Michel Vallon glanced from one to the other and said, 'We are very glad to have you. Without the British women volunteers our medical services would be completely over-whelmed.'

'Thank you,' said Merle. She paused and then spoke distinctly in French. 'We're expecting to be kept *pretty* busy. And we appreciate that wounded men are not a *pretty* sight, but we're *pretty* much prepared for anything we may have to cope with.'

There was a short silence before Michel Vallon clicked his tongue against his teeth and declared, 'Ah! The bar!'

With deep satisfaction Merle saw Captain George Taylor's face blush crimson.

Grace leaned forward. 'Is there a joke that I am missing?'

Michel Vallon chuckled. 'One might say *un esprit d'escalier*. Miss Stevenson will explain later, I'm sure.'

He tilted his head towards Merle. 'Where did you learn your French?'

'From my *maman*,' Merle answered him. 'My home was in Paris until my parents were killed in a road accident when I was seven years old. My father was British and I was sent to live with his mother as my own had no relatives who could take me in. This is the first time I've been back.'

'How sad to lose one's parents when so young.'

'Yes, it was,' Merle agreed. 'And it took me months to bond with my grandmother. But now we are very close. She's the reason I'm here. She is a friend of Doctor Elsie Inglis, who started the Scottish Women's Hospitals for Foreign Service.' She shot a look at Captain Taylor. 'All the staff are women: doctors, nurses, cooks and ambulance drivers. After reading her letters about the conditions of the soldiers, I felt I must do something to help.'

'Bravo!' Michel raised his glass. 'Bravo to you both, Miss Merle Stevenson and Miss Grace Jeffries.'

'Yes, indeed!' Captain Taylor quickly raised his glass. 'Miss Stevenson, regarding what happened earlier, I must say—'

'No, you must not,' Michel Vallon placed his hand on the captain's arm. 'Not here and not now. At a future date you may sue for peace with Miss Stevenson, and I hope you will be successful. But for the moment we will talk of pleasant things and avoid discord of any kind.'

When Merle awoke early the next day there was a folded

piece of paper pushed under the door of the room she was sharing with Grace. She picked it up and read:

Dear Miss Stevenson,

I am so terribly sorry that I offended you.
Please try to forgive my foolish remarks. They were not intended for you to hear – although I appreciate that in itself is no excuse.
I spoke out of ignorance and thoughtlessness, and hope that you will overlook my abominable bad manners.

Yours sincerely,
Captain George Taylor

Merle pushed the note into the pocket of her coat. She would decide later if she would forgive him. For this hour before breakfast she wanted to be outside with her drawing materials.

It was a bleak November morning, but the docks were busy. America had recently joined the War on the side of the Allies and already ships loaded with troops and supplies were arriving. Merle had to walk far along the promenade to find a quiet place to work. Her mother had once taken her to see the *Mona Lisa* and explained da Vinci's use of shadow and light. It was the year prior to the accident, so Merle could only have been about six or seven, but she recalled it vividly. Maman holding her in her arms so that she could peer more closely at the face in the painting. '*Sfumato*,' Maman said. 'Like smoke. That's what it's called when the painter uses this technique. There's always light in the shadow.'

She had loved the *Mona Lisa* as she had loved all paintings, the Old Masters and newer artists like the Impressionists. She especially adored van Gogh, with his achingly vibrant canvases.

Merle put up her folding stool and easel by the sea wall. Dawn was etching the sky with slices of pearl and pewter. She sensed the colours unfold within her as she painted.

As she reached round for a cloth to wipe her brush, she found, instead, the golden-haired captain. How long had he been standing there? In the daylight she saw he wasn't much older than she was. A tiny frown appeared on her forehead. She hated having her concentration disturbed. She wasn't privileged enough to be a Government-commissioned war artist – it was almost exclusively men who held those posts – so every moment of her spare time was precious.

'Good morning.'

Merle nodded.

'Perhaps we may speak later?'

'Perhaps,' she said

'I'll not distract you.' He touched his fingers to his cap and walked back the way he had come. A decent distance away he sat down upon a bench, opened a book and began to read.

Twenty minutes elapsed without him turning a page. Merle allowed herself a smile. She continued working for the best part of an hour before she conceded that in punishing him she was punishing herself, for the weather wasn't warm and her coat was thin.

As she started to gather her belongings he leaped to his feet and approached. 'May I help you?' he asked politely.

'I am perfectly capable of carrying my own things,' she replied.

'Truthfully I didn't seek you out in order to offer to help carry your bag,' he said. 'I wanted to apologise again for my behaviour last night.'

When she didn't reply, he went on. 'I am mortified.'

'It was an arrogant remark,' she said finally.

'It was,' he admitted, 'and stupid too. I displeased the French Red Cross officer whom I am supposed to be helping. I am co-ordinating the hospital trains in his sector,' he explained.

'You assumed that, as females, we would not speak French, not be capable of knowing any language other than English.'

'I cannot claim even that amount of thought. It was a silly joke, and I didn't think of the consequences. I have no experience of women, being an only child whose mother died when I was born. I've no girl cousins either to teach me how to be less awkward and clumsy. I am truly sorry.'

Merle saw that he was making banter in order to win her over. She hesitated to let him off so easily, until he added,

'I have just got my commission and I am overexcited at being here at last, and, truth to tell, somewhat nervous.'

'Are you?' Merle scanned his face. Something in his eyes told her this was the truth, and it had cost him a tiny part of himself to admit it to her – maybe he was only now admitting it to himself?

'But I did think I might be of use to you this morning.'

'In what way?' Merle slung the satchel over her shoulder and picked up her easel and stool to let him see that she could manage on her own.

'With this.' He took a napkin from his pocket and unwrapped it. 'I feared you'd miss breakfast so I brought you a bread roll with some jam. If you accept it I will see it as a sign that you've forgiven me.'

Merle put her hand out for the roll.

'I'm so glad.' George Taylor grinned at her. 'For we are travelling together today and it would be intolerable if we were not speaking to each other.'

That afternoon the two new ambulances set off south to Trécourt, bumping over long cobbled avenues lined with poplar trees. On the open road the booming of heavy guns sounded louder.

They stopped in a village. The streets were empty, many of the inhabitants having fled west, in fear of being overrun if the Germans broke through. Unbelievably there was a café open. The owner made them hot chocolate, which she'd saved for just such an occasion, she told them. She would accept no payment. 'I have two sons fighting. I haven't heard from them in over a year. If you meet them, tell them their mother loves them and she is waiting for them at home.'

They stretched their legs before continuing and Merle wandered into a nearby orchard. The trees were still bearing fruit, as if reluctant to surrender to winter. Yellow, garnet and gold; the canopy above her was the smudged paintbox of autumn.

Her grandmother had come home unexpectedly early on the day of the caning. The front door slamming made the governess jump. She thrust the cane at the housemaid. 'Return that to where it belongs.'

The maid put her hands behind her back.

Merle clenched her teeth, determined not to cry.

And that was the scene which greeted her grandmother as she swept into the room, removing pins from her hat as she came. She tossed it onto a sofa and paused in the act of unbuttoning her gloves.

'What's amiss?'

'This miss is amiss.' The governess gave a harsh laugh.

Merle watched the feather of her grandmother's hat waft gently to and fro. A magnificent purple feather, fastened with the white, green and violet ribbons of the women's suffrage movement.

'How so?' Her grandmother's eyes narrowed as she took in the cane in the governess's hand.

'I find the girl's nature very obdurate. I drew specific trees for her to colour in. I even placed the crayons in order, so she would not have to think too much. See for yourself what she has done!' The governess's voice railed with righteous indignation. 'She broke every crayon. On purpose! Then she made a mess of the outlines.'

'Did you ask her why?'

'There is no point in asking her why. Children are born with a wickedness in them that needs to be driven out.'

'Oh, I think there is always a point in asking why.' Merle's grandmother sat down on the chair opposite her. 'Would you like to tell me why you broke the crayons?'

Merle shook her head.

'Ma'am,' the housemaid began, 'she's a wee girl in a strange country and—'

Merle's grandmother held up her hand. 'I'd like Merle herself to tell me. Please. *S'il vous plaît.*' And, as the child's gaze flickered to her face, she smiled and winked at her.

'They are too big for my hand.'

'Nonsense!' the governess said. 'She uses her slate pencil quite easily and that is longer than these crayons.'

'I write with the pencil,' said Merle. 'With crayons, I draw.'

'Show me,' her grandmother prompted.

Merle gripped the stub of a crayon in her fist and slid it on its side across the paper.

'You see how ridiculous that is?' said the governess. 'One cannot possibly colour in properly using a crayon that way.'

'What were you drawing, *ma petite*?'

Merle pointed to the garden where the evening sun, coming through the overhanging branches, had created a cave of colour. 'Trees,' she said. 'I draw trees.'

'That's unlike any tree I've ever seen,' the governess snorted. 'There's no form, no lines.'

Merle's grandmother studied the multi-toned splashes of apricot and orange on the paper, the kaleidoscope of hues, the iridescent blend of rose-tinted cream overlapping brown and black to create warmth within shade. Then she stared out of the window into the garden, glowing with dappled light of russet, ochre, amber and yellow.

'My granddaughter does not constrict herself to lines,' she said. 'Merle is drawing Life.'

'I cannot teach a girl who will not obey a simple instruction.'

'It's perceptive of you to acknowledge that you cannot teach,' said her grandmother, 'because a true teacher would know that girls should be taught to think for themselves.'

The following morning the governess was gone. The next week her grandmother engaged a drawing instructor and proudly accompanied Merle when, in her early teens, she enrolled as one of the youngest students at the Edinburgh College of Art.

When they reached Trécourt the staff were wearing black mourning armbands. Doctor Elsie Inglis, who had been suffering from cancer, had died on the twenty-sixth of

November, the day after coming back to England from the hospital she'd established in Serbia.

Everyone assembled in the dining hall, where the supervisor of Trécourt Ambulance Station, Mrs Anne Thomson, read a lesson, and begged them not to be disheartened.

'Doctor Inglis would have wanted us to carry on her good work. We aren't a large unit here, unlike the main hospitals run by women at Abbaye de Royaumont and Villers-Cotterêts, but, being close to the railway, our work is crucial in ferrying the wounded to where they need to go.'

The two new ambulances brought the number up to five, with ten drivers, including Merle and Grace. Mrs Thomson ran the unit, arranging staff shifts and ordering supplies. The work was unrelenting. The phone would ring or a bicycle messenger would bring word that a hospital train was due at the railway depot. Off they would go, backwards and forwards, shuttling the men to their designated hospitals. If they weren't driving, they took their turn at cooking and cleaning, and, above everything else, ensuring the vans were ready for action. They slept on mattresses made from jute bags stuffed with hay and lugged sacks of anthracite from the coal store to fuel the stoves to keep themselves warm. There was little free time but Merle managed to draw or paint fairly regularly. As long as it did not interfere with the function of the unit the supervisor thought it an excellent idea to record their activities.

Merle painted everything she saw: wounded soldiers with officers and orderlies moving amongst them; a doctor speaking to one of her patients; the ambulances, inside and out; Grace with engine parts spread around her; the girls working, eating or writing letters home. She was convinced of the importance of art in this context and it fulfilled a need within her, making Merle more content than she'd felt for years. She was allowed to make a studio in one of the attic rooms, and it was there Captain George Taylor found her one day when he came to call.

'It's marvellous how you reveal colour in a winter land-scape,' he said, examining her painting of two women standing in snow under a tree. 'You have infused light into the barren branches.'

'You sound knowledgeable about art,' said Merle. 'Do you paint?'

'I did dabble. My art master said that I had a talent, but perhaps that was merely to keep himself employed.'

Merle clipped fresh paper onto the easel and handed him a brush. With deft strokes he painted her standing beside her ambulance.

'An accomplished representation,' she said sincerely.

'Mmm...' He glanced from his painting to hers, now drying on the window shelf. 'I'm more interested in what you're doing with colour. At some point I will ask you to show me how you achieve those effects.'

It was nearly Christmas before Merle saw George Taylor

again. She and Grace had gone into Albert, a town east of Trécourt. They had decided to have their hair cut short. Most of the other drivers had done this already. It reduced the incidence of lice and made shampooing cheaper and faster. By chance they met George, who was in search of a new razor.

'It's so tedious to have to shave every day,' he confided.

The girls sympathised and explained the problems of long hair.

'Oh, surely not!' he said when they told him of their intention to have it cut. 'Ladies' hair is a joy to behold. If one is allowed to make that comment,' he added.

'We might have to report you to Supervisor Thomson,' joked Grace.

But Mrs Thomson was an admirer of Captain Taylor and had invited him as a guest to their Christmas dinner. 'Since that young man was appointed,' she said, 'patient transport is more efficient.'

On Christmas Day he arrived at the unit in full dress uniform, which Merle deduced was borrowed, because it hung loose on his body and long in the sleeve.

'He is attractive,' murmured Grace, 'you must admit.'

'I'm not admitting to anything,' said Merle, but she was laughing. Conversation was certainly less strained than the last dinner they'd eaten together.

It was clear that Michel Vallon had also changed his opinion about Captain Taylor. During the meal he spoke warmly of the young officer's re-organisation. Extra spur lines accommodated the trains coming and going. Through-out the journey wounds were assessed and a medical card pinned to each man. An up-to-date tally was kept on the sector's operating theatre and bed availability. It meant savings in time and fuel, because patients were taken directly to the most appropriate hospital or surgical unit.

'When the war is over,' Monsieur Vallon promised, 'I intend to recommend Captain Taylor for the *Légion d'honneur*.'

'When do you think that will be?' asked Grace. 'We hear conflicting reports. The official Allied bulletins are very positive, yet our patients tell us a different story.'

'It will be months yet,' said Michel, 'but we *will* win.'

Merle saw George look away as the older man said this. 'We are not children to be reassured with half-truths,' she said.

'It would be better if you were open with us,' agreed Supervisor Thomson. 'For if there is any doubt, then we should practise our evacuation drill more often.'

'It would be a wise precaution.' George spoke very defi-nitely. 'We are vulnerable in this sector. Fewer trenches have been built for defence and it has left the town of Albert and the surrounding area exposed.'

'But I've heard you say that trench warfare is a vile stalemate,' said Merle.

'It is, but at least it affords some protection for those behind the line.'

* * *

As the new year began, so did the rumours.

'A patient I was transporting today said that the German army have been amassing reinforcements,' one of the drivers announced at dinner.

'Reinforcements?' Grace was astonished. 'How can they possibly have reinforcements?'

'I fear it is true,' said Supervisor Thomson. 'Their elite forces have been recalled from the Russian Front. They may be planning a spring offensive.'

'I heard that too.' Another girl spoke up. 'A doctor on the last train I picked up from mentioned heavy artillery and stormtroopers carrying flamethrowers.'

Supervisor Thomson gave the girl a severe look. 'Let's not spread alarm. We will be ready to evacuate at a moment's notice, but we must continue to provide an ambulance service for as long as we are able.'

At the supervisor's instruction, they each packed a minimum of personal things and put them in the ambulances so that, if it became necessary, they could leave the base at once. Merle placed her paintings in her satchel and stowed it in her van. She remembered what George had said about this area being vulnerable. If the enemy did start to use long-range guns then Albert would be the target. She opened up the map she always carried in her coat pocket.

Albert – only a few miles east of Trécourt.

The bomb landed without warning.

Above the clatter of the engine Merle didn't hear the

whine of its approach. One moment she was on a country road, almost empty apart from a group of soldiers standing outside their billet. The next moment there was a bang that shut off her hearing and seventy yards in front of her the earth erupted. The van rocked, steadied, and then – it seemed as if in slow motion – a torrent of stones and debris rained out of the sky. Rocks bounced off the roof and she was thrown forward. She hit the brake and skidded to a halt.

Silence. Cries for help. Orders being shouted.

Legs trembling, Merle got out of the van. Her first instinct was to crouch down and check that the tyres were intact.

'Thank God! There's an ambulance!' Someone pulled at her arm. 'You got stretchers in there, buddy?'

She straightened up to face an American Army Sergeant.

'Save my stars!' he cried. 'The driver's a girl!'

'Do you want me or not?' Merle snapped. 'I'll drive on somewhere else if I'm not welcome here.'

'You tell him, hen!' said one of his men in a familiar broad accent. 'He's too crabbit, by far.'

'You're welcome. You're welcome,' the sergeant told her. 'I'd lay the table for afternoon tea to show how welcome you are, but first I need to dig my boys out of that mess.'

'All right!' Merle was half laughing, half sobbing. 'I'll get the stretchers from my van.'

They worked for an hour pulling bodies from the rubble. Of the group of twenty men in and around the shattered building, only four were alive. The last one, a boy, who looked about fifteen years old, they dug out with their bare hands. His pelvis and legs were crushed.

With horn blaring, Merle drove to the nearest hospital. She jumped from the cab as the staff came running.

'Unclassified wounded. Bomb hit on a US army billet. Four patients,' Merle gasped out to the admitting nurse as she opened the ambulance doors. 'This boy. This one here. The young one. His sergeant wants you to look at him first.'

The nurse gave the boy a quick examination and beckoned Merle to one side.

'He's dying. It's not worth moving him. We'll admit the others and let him pass away here.'

'What can I do?' Merle asked desperately.

'There's nothing you can do except comfort him.'

'What do I say?' she asked, but the nurse had left, hurrying after the three casualties who were being carried inside.

Merle got into the back of her ambulance.

'They've not forgotten about me, have they?' the boy asked her.

'No, no, of course not.' Merle thought quickly. 'They've gone to get you morphine.'

'Funny thing. I told the sergeant as he was digging me out, I'm not in pain. No pain at all.'

'That's good then. The hospital's short of morphine. But you Americans are in the war now. And you've got supplies.' Merle realised she was babbling but couldn't stop. 'I saw them being unloaded at Calais when I was there.'

'I'm just a bit cold.'

Merle took off her coat and spread it across his body. 'Better now?'

He nodded. Then he said in a low voice, 'I'm a bit frightened too. Didn't like to say it in front of the sergeant, but you're a girl so I reckon it's OK for you to know.'

'Oh, everyone gets scared.'

'Really?'

'Oh, yes. I've had every rank in this ambulance. Majors, brigadiers, generals, the lot. Shaking like jellies they were. Getting wounded is very scary. . .' Merle's voice trailed off. The boy's face had turned a colour she had never seen before.

'I'm dying, aren't I?' The boy was struggling for breath now, the air rattling in his chest.

Merle felt panic rising in her. She didn't know how to deal with this. That was why she'd elected to be a driver. It was all very well for the nurse to say 'comfort him', but how was she supposed to do that?

His eyes were shading into pools of darkness.

With sudden inspiration Merle remembered the woman in the café of the village where she and Grace and Captain Taylor had stopped for lunch on their drive south. She kneeled down beside the dying boy. 'Your mother loves you,' she whispered. 'She loves you very much.'

The boy relaxed. He closed his eyes and quietly sighed his last breath.

Merle stood up. There was a hard, tight pain across her chest. She stumbled out and climbed into the cabin. She bowed her head to rest it on the wheel as the stretcher-bearers took the boy to the mortuary.

The next day she couldn't paint, nor the day after, nor the day after that.

Sfumato ...

There was no light in the shadows.

She did her work automatically and thought only in monochrome. Grace and the other girls tried to cheer her. Mrs Thomson was sympathetic and supportive. 'A first death is always hard. Take some time to be in the fresh air.'

Merle walked aimlessly. The sights of conflict – the ruined houses and despoiled earth – filled her waking moments, and at night the rumble of the guns disturbed her dreams. She began to believe that her presence in the ambulance unit would make no difference to the outcome of this terrible war, and concluded that she could not exist in a landscape where all forms of life were constantly under assault.

She'd made up her mind that she would return to Edinburgh when George appeared. There was excitement in his face. 'You must come with me. I have found treasure.'

Reluctantly she followed him. It was kind of him to try to raise her spirits, but there was nothing she could think of that would ease the gloom that enveloped her.

He took her into the barn where the coal was stored and stopped in front of a ladder that led to the hayloft.

'Up here?' Merle stared at him.

'Yes,' he said, 'there is something I want you to see.'

She did as he said, and, as her eyes came level with the rafters, Merle saw a bird's nest tucked in the crossbeam. Three speckled turquoise eggs lay snug among the twigs.

'Isn't it beautiful?' George asked softly. 'A miracle of engineering that has life within it.'

Merle gazed at the nest.

'I can tell by the eggs that it's the nest of a blackbird,' he said.

Tears prickled Merle's eyelids.

'You understand why I brought you here?'

Merle nodded, not trusting herself to speak.

> *Chante, chante,*
> *Petit oiseau,*
> *Chante pour moi,*
> *Mon petit merle.*

She was with her parents in a park, skipping on the grass as they sang her special song. Her father caught her and lifted her high in the air. 'Come and kiss me, my Merle, my bonnie little blackbird.'

Merle. Her name in French meant blackbird.

The chicks began to hatch in early March. Merle drew them as fledglings, hopping about among the red poppies and *les bleuets*, the bright blue cornflowers. Mrs Thomson watched her paint. She put her hand on Merle's shoulder. 'It's ironic that some plants thrive in soil that has been displaced. Due to the devastation around us, these flowers bloom more profusely, yet I find their tenacity and beauty uplifting.'

On a fine spring morning two weeks later they received an order to move the ambulance base to Amiens. They were expected there the next day. The girls were beginning to check the engines and load the vans with supplies when George's truck hurtled into the yard.

'Albert has fallen! You must leave immediately!'

Supervisor Thomson was a calm, practical woman. Within minutes the unit was lined up to go. 'Keep as close as possible to the vehicle in front and only sound the horn if absolutely necessary. I will be in the lead ambulance. Captain Taylor, would you like to travel at the rear?'

'I cannot go with you,' said George. 'There's a hospital train on its way down here. I need to drive to the unmanned signal box at Fernaut and change the points to re-route it north-west.'

'But that means driving towards Albert!' Merle could not keep the concern from her voice.

George was already walking towards his truck. Supervisor Thomson called after him. 'Captain Taylor, I suppose you are aware that Fernaut is directly in the path of the enemy advance?'

'I am aware of that fact. But I am also aware of my duty to try to protect the hospital train. Your ambulances don't move as fast as my truck. I'll wager I can change the points at Fernaut and catch up with you before you reach Amiens.'

'He shouldn't go alone.' Merle turned to her supervisor. 'I'd like to go with Captain Taylor.'

'You certainly will not.' George's reply was abrupt.

'Why do you say that?' Mrs Thomson asked him. 'Common sense dictates that two people are more likely to succeed.'

'We don't put our women in the Front Line...'

'War has put us where we are, and we women must also do our duty as we see it. This is an emergency situation. Miss Stevenson is an experienced motor driver with some medical qualifications, who has shown she can operate in extreme conditions. She'd be an asset on your mission. The personal documents carried by Miss Stevenson identify her as Red Cross personnel. If captured, her safety is guaranteed by International Law.'

Merle rushed to hug Grace and was in the passenger seat of the truck as her supervisor finished speaking. Silently George got in beside her and drove away from the base.

It was only when the signal box came into view that George eventually spoke to her. In a tight voice he said, 'You are a very determined woman, Miss Stevenson.'

Merle thought it best not to reply.

'And brave too.'

At Fernaut, George parked the truck and they crossed the railway tracks and climbed up to the box. The crash of artillery was the loudest Merle had ever heard – and it was coming closer. From their vantage point they could see the sky in the east livid with flame. They could also see the train snaking its way towards them.

George had been given a set of written instructions by the manager of the railway depot, who had elected to remain behind to facilitate any Allied retreat movements. George moved the levers as Merle read the instructions aloud.

'The train should come past us and then veer right towards Abbeville,' George told her. 'We'll get back in the truck and watch it go.'

The sniper caught them as they were re-crossing the railway line. A flick of wind and a double snap of sound. George's body jerked. He staggered and fell. Merle flung herself flat on the ground. The bullet had entered above his right elbow and exited through his hand. His fingers were a pulp of blood and broken bone. Merle pulled out the emergency dressing she kept in her pocket and tied it round his wound.

Beneath them the tracks were vibrating with the approach of the train, but he made no attempt to move. She looked at him. Blood was oozing from a tear in his trouser leg. There had been two rifle reports. He'd been shot twice and couldn't stand up. He was grimacing in pain, but still lucid. 'Go!' he ordered her.

'No.'

'Please.'

'No,' she said again. The rails were thrumming all along the line.

'I can't get on my feet.'

'You can crawl.' She spoke in the firm, encouraging tone she'd heard nurses use with patients half mad with shell shock. 'Together we can crawl off this track.'

He put his arm round her shoulder and pushed down with his unharmed foot to help her as she hauled him over the first rail. 'One more and we're there,' she said. 'Come on!' With a huge effort she heaved him up and onto the cinder at the edge of the track.

The train was upon them, their faces inches from the wheels as it roared past.

'We have to hurry!' Merle shouted in his ear. The sniper was on the signal-box side of the track. The passing train was shielding them from him – but only for another few seconds.

Half dragging him, she got to the truck and hefted him up inside. She started the engine. The last carriage went past and the train veered off on its altered course towards the north. She engaged the clutch and they rocketed forwards onto the road to Amiens.

The Germans must be moving forward very fast, she thought. The air shook as the shells flew overhead, followed by a resounding crump and a shudder. Where were they landing? There had been talk that the enemy had a gun with enough power to hit Paris. They had sent snipers on ahead...and what else? Merle forced the thought of flamethrowers from her mind. She positioned the truck in the middle of the road and vowed nothing would stop her.

She kept talking to George to keep him awake and conscious. He was propped against the passenger door, but she knew that he was losing blood and probably going into shock. She gabbled on about her life. She asked him questions about his own. Now she could see the outskirts of the town, the sandbagged defences. Almost there!

Then she heard the buzz of an aeroplane above and behind her.

Merle guessed what the pilot was doing – signalling to his own artillery the location of the Amiens gun emplacements. He swooped low so that she would see him. She'd heard that the airmen were disinclined to strafe running men and if she got out he'd see that she wasn't a combatant. She glanced at George. His head was slumped on his chest. He couldn't run anywhere, and even if she could help him down from the cab in time, he wouldn't be capable of walking to Amiens. His only chance was if she could reach the city in the truck. She put her foot on the accelerator pedal and pressed it to the floor.

The pilot gained height to bank, change direction and line himself up with his target.

Merle watched the plane begin its manoeuvre and saw the pilot's intention. On an impulse she swung the truck over to one side of the road. Not much of an edge, but better than nothing.

The pilot centred the crosshairs and began his run in. The plane came screaming towards the truck. Merle held her nerve. As the pilot opened fire she spun the wheel and slewed across the road. The windscreen cracked, bullets battered the outside plating. But she was still driving. She was still driving! It would take the plane several minutes to return, but there was the city and the outward defence posts, and there were soldiers – Allied soldiers, waving frantically at her. She was clear. She had made it through. She was close enough now to hear them yelling, to hear what they were saying: 'Incoming shells! Incoming shells! Get off the road! Get off the road!'

Merle wrenched the wheel round.

Twenty seconds too late.

She awoke to find Grace sitting by her bed, holding her hand.

'You've been out for almost ten days,' she said. 'Concussion, broken ribs, multiple abrasions.'

Merle had no memory of what had happened. Her only recollection was of a blinding white light, and then utter darkness. 'And George?' She was frightened to say his name. 'How is George?'

'He's alive.'

Merle began to cry. Grace stroked her forehead until she fell asleep.

Weeks passed while Merle slowly became fully aware of the world around her and could absorb the information Grace brought. The Allies had stopped the enemy advance outside Amiens. The German supply line was so far to their rear that it could no longer support their forward troops.

Although Albert was still being looted, they were running out of food and ammunition.

'Intelligence reports say that the ordinary soldier wants peace,' said Grace. 'It's estimated that, by summer, their commanders will ask to agree an armistice.'

They were back in Calais where George was having specialist dental surgery.

'The right side of his face, his cheek and jaw, are smashed,' Grace told Merle. 'He's lost the three middle digits from his right hand. And . . .' She hesitated.

'And, what?' Merle looked at her friend. 'We've been through so much together. Please tell me the truth.'

'Between operations he's being treated by a psychiatrist,' said Grace. 'He's very depressed. He doesn't sleep well, barely eats.'

When she was well enough to walk, Merle collected her drawing satchel from Grace and went to visit George.

'They tell me that you're in a sorry state,' she said as she sat down beside his bed.

The nurse drew in her breath and gave Merle a sharp look before she left them.

'Not a pretty sight,' George joked, but there were tears in his eyes.

'You did say that you found shaving tiresome.' Merle gestured with her hand. 'You must grow a beard.'

'And that takes care of things, does it?' he asked. 'You think I'll look as good as new with a beard?'

Merle studied his face. 'You might look even better, if it's the same colour as your hair,' she said softly. 'I've always wanted to capture that particular shade of gold.'

There was a silence in the room. Merle held George's gaze.

'And this?' He held up his right hand, which had only a little finger and thumb. 'What do I do with this?'

Merle opened her satchel. She took out her drawing chalks and scattered them over his bedcovers. Then, one by one, she began to snap them in half.

Ghost Story
by Matt Whyman

Ghost Story

In 1915, with the Western Front in stalemate, the Allies turned their attention to the Black Sea. This largely landlocked ocean is linked to the Aegean Sea, and the Atlantic beyond, by a narrow strait through Turkey. By taking out the Turks as they prepared to back Germany in the war effort, the Allies believed they could free up access to vital grain stores mounting in the Russian ports of Odessa, Sevastopol and Feodosia.

The Gallipoli peninsula forms one side of the strait. Despite the rough and inhospitable terrain, where beaches fronted steep ridges, the Allies believed that victory here would be easy. What they underestimated was the fierce determination of the Turkish army.

Despite the aid of naval bombardments, the Australian, New Zealand and British troops were forced, on landing, into a siege that proved impossible to break. As a consequence, the campaign proved to be one of the greatest disasters of the First World War. Over half a million soldiers from both sides lost their lives in the nine months before the Allies finally withdrew, with many dying from disease.

On their return from Gallipoli, some Allied soldiers claimed that they had come under fire from female snipers. Their testimonies are heartfelt and compelling, even if historians counter that the facts have been lost to the fog of war. With no evidence beyond eyewitness accounts, we can only imagine what might have led a markswoman to emerge on the front line.

We are like birds perched in the pine trees. Unlike the sparrows and the siskins, however, we are silent. When we sing, we will do so with a bullet.

My fellow sniper, up here in the branches, is more of a boy than a man. I am old enough to be his mother. Not that I can say for sure Timur knows the truth about me. Through his eyes, I might be just another soldier in an army that will fight to the death to protect Turkish land. Defeat is not in our nature. Sacrifice is all, and I have already crossed that line.

'They are close,' he whispers urgently, and then gestures at the farmhouse in the clearing beyond the trees. 'You were right!'

I do not reply. Timur can see that I have heard him because I peer down the sights of my rifle. The dwelling has been shelled. It used to be a secure and comfortable place to live. I know this for a fact because once it was my home. Not any more. To lose one family member in battle is a tragedy. To lose two means *war*. So now I look at the place in a different light. Through enemy eyes, those of the soldiers seeking to push inland. I have no doubt that they will be drawn inside.

After months of existing in a rat run of trenches and channels, even a derelict building will appear enticing. It also provides me with the perfect lure to bring them into my crosshair.

Before the first figure emerges from the thicket on the far side of the clearing, the crackle of twigs gives away his position. I find the soldier in my sights as he crawls into the sunshine, but do not shoot. My companion and I have agreed a procedure to ensure the highest kill count. The Allies took the lives of my husband and then my son in the space of a month. They did not leave behind a widow, however. They awakened a warrior.

I had been staying with my cousin, some miles from the front line, when news arrived that there was nothing more for me to lose. She collapsed on hearing that my dear boy had fallen, just as I had when I learned that his father had died. This time, I felt nothing. I had already been through every emotion within the spectrum of grief. My heart and soul had perished with my family, which is when I made the decision to return home.

When the Allies landed on our shores, and looked up the scarps, it seemed they thought the climb would be their greatest challenge. Instead, our troops have been courageous in keeping them pinned to the slopes and the beach. Of course, the enemy reacted like a trapped wildcat. For months they have fought to break through, probing every gulley and gorge, and then mounting assaults through day and night, but we continue to hound them ferociously.

The crackle of gunfire grew more intense as I drifted back. It was chaos, with the walking wounded urging me to turn around. The front line was no place for a woman, they said. It was no place for anyone, I thought to myself, and continued on my way. I could have claimed to be delivering munitions and supplies like so many other girls who refused to stay away. Instead, I just ignored such questioning and drifted on. Quite simply, I was compelled to be in the place where my family once felt safe. I didn't flinch or cower at the howl of mortars launching. I was already dead in my mind. Among those who witnessed me as I floated by, always looking straight ahead, some would've been forgiven for thinking they had witnessed a wraith.

By early afternoon, I had reached forested slopes. It was cooler under the canopy of branches and leaves, while the moths and dragonflies that flitted through the beams of light were at odds with the din. From the other side of the ridge, the crackle of traded shots told me just how close I had come to the front line. Here, the two sides had dug in, facing one another in a ragged ribbon that ran for mile upon mile along the peninsula. Death had come to dwell here, striking as mercilessly as the mosquitoes, and yet I gave no thought to my welfare. I just followed a path through the trees that I knew would take me to the farmhouse. My determination to reach home grew stronger with every step. Despite the dangers, it was all I wanted. I had no plans beyond this, until something stopped me in my tracks as if presented from on high.

The body, when I came across it, was enshrouded by blowflies. The way the soldier was sprawled under the tree, with his limbs at odds with their joints and his cap some distance across the forest floor, made it quite clear that he had fallen from the branches. The bullet wound to his neck told me what had prompted him to drop. That the blood was still slick suggested that this had happened only recently. His nose and mouth were obscured by a cotton scarf but I could see through the glaze in his eyes that this was just a boy. Another son now lost to us all, and I looked upon him as a mother in spirit. For the first time since I had left my cousin's home, I sensed an emotion rise within me; an anger that lifted the hairs on the back of my neck.

The soldier wore a tunic fashioned from a rough green blanket, daubed in mud just like his face and tied round his waist with a belt. A sniper rifle lay just beyond his reach, bound in filthy strips of cotton to dull the gleam. I peered up and around. The trees overlooked a ravine with a narrow view of the sea beyond. From the canopy, it offered a clear shot at the enemy should they seek to push forward from the shoreline. I returned my attention to the ground. Slowly, despite the malevolent buzzing all around, I dropped to my knees and prepared to honour the boy by laying him to rest.

When I finally continued on my way, I left behind a mound of dried leaves and twigs that I had swept together using my hands. It was the best I could do under the circum-stances. I carried the rifle over my shoulder. In the pocket of the tunic, which I had pulled on, I found a box of bullets. With the scarf around my nose and mouth, and my hair tucked tightly under the cap, I didn't just feel different in my appearance. Where there had been nothing in my mind beyond an instinct to go home, I walked now with a sense of determination. The boots were too big for me, of course, but I refused to falter. With the blanket, scarf and rifle, even the soil I had scrubbed across my face to complete my camouflage, it felt as if I carried the soul not just of the fallen soldier but all those who had died for this cause, including my husband and son. It meant I had memories for company, which served as both a torment and a blessing.

My poor boy was uppermost in my mind when I heard sobbing. The sound was clear despite the gunfire over the ridge, and evidently close by. Immediately, I dropped out of sight in the bracken. When I heard it again, someone trying hard to stifle their emotions, I crawled towards the source. In a glade to my right, I saw a young soldier sitting with his back to a tree and a long rifle across his lap. He kept rubbing his face with both hands; angered, it seemed, by his loss of composure. Like the boy I had buried not thirty yards back, he used a muddy green blanket to blend into the foliage. Straight away, I knew he had just lost a companion.

Mindful not to startle him, I retreated from the glade. Only then, when I felt sure that he could not see me, did I make my presence known.

'If I was the enemy,' I called out, 'my voice would be the last you ever heard in this world.'

'Who is there?' The boy scrambled to his feet. At the same time, while frantically looking one way and then the other, he let the rifle drop and snatched a pistol from his belt. 'Identify yourself!' he cried.

'A fellow patriot.' Setting my rifle on the ground, I made a decision in that moment to trust the soldier with my life. I had spoken with a deliberate gruffness, but there was no threat in my tone. Slowly, I emerged from behind the bracken, my hands held high. The boy looked stunned. He took a step back, dropping his pistol to his side and then stood and simply stared at me. Carefully, I lowered my arms and spread my hands. 'I am here for you,' I added.

'Zeki?' He sounded shocked and uncertain. 'It's me, Timur!' he crowed. 'My God!'

In a blink, I realised what conclusion he had drawn. The boy looked tormented, not just, I supposed, by the apparent resurrection of his friend but by the constant shelling and shooting. It was some way off, but sounded wholly unpredictable, as if we could be engulfed at any moment. I drew breath to explain myself, and then thought better of it.

'It isn't safe here,' I said, keeping my voice low and quiet, and then gestured at the path I had been following. 'But I know of a place close by where we will have the upper hand.'

Timur asked no further questions. He simply trailed behind me to the edge of the forest. I chose not to engage him in conversation, unwilling to turn and let him look me in the eye. But as we progressed, I decided he must have come to recognise I was not the young man he had declared me to be in the shock of that moment. Despite being wrapped in the thick tunic, which hid my body shape, my frame was slight compared to his former companion's. We spoke the same language, of course, which must have assured him that we were fighting for a common cause. Still, he didn't press me once. Even if the young man had worked out that he was in the company of a woman, perhaps my true identity was not as important to him as the fact that another human being had taken him under wing.

'Thank you,' I heard him whisper at one point, though I did not reply.

On seeing the first glimpse of my former home, there beyond the foliage, my emotions surged again. I'd carried a sense of anger here since finding the body of the fallen soldier. Now I felt silent outrage at what I saw before me. With the roof collapsed into the rooms below, the place was barely recognisable. My memories of the years we had lived there as a family remained vivid, but what I faced felt like something that should be forgotten. They say you should fight for your country, but it was the life I'd lost with my family that drove me onwards. I felt no sentimentality. It was time to take a stand.

I turned to Timur. For the first time, I let him look me in the eyes. Even with the scarf around his mouth and nose, I saw no sense of surprise, just an air of apprehension as to why I had led him to this spot.

'I always believed that I would end my days here,' I told him.

Timur blinked, and considered what I had said. Briefly, he glanced back at the ruins of the farmhouse. When his gaze came back to me, I knew he understood just what I meant.

'I'm sorry for your loss,' he said, and bowed his head.

Now it was my turn to look again upon the stricken building. If it had once been a place of love and laughter, the ruins would soon come to serve a completely different purpose. I took a step back and looked upwards. Here stood pines so dense that the branches of each tree meshed with the next.

'In time they will come to this place,' I told Timur. 'And when they do, we shall be ready.' I gestured at the canopy overhead. 'We can position ourselves far apart or we can operate together.'

Timur looked at me. 'Together,' he said with some certainty. 'We should watch out for each other.'

I guessed that Timur and Zeki had worked from different vantage points. This had probably saved Timur's life. Sniping in close proximity would double our vulnerability. But it was clear to me that my new companion had no further wish to be alone.

We began to climb. Watching Timur find a handhold on the lower branch, and then carefully work his way up the tree, I wondered whether he had ever used the rifle issued to him. He seemed so uncomfortable with it strapped to his back, as if it had been forced upon him. He could certainly climb without difficulty, which was probably a skill he'd picked up in childhood. Firing a weapon was a very different challenge; the same one I faced myself. My husband had owned a shotgun to keep the rabbits at bay. I had never even held it, let alone pulled a trigger, nor had I felt any desire to do so. In a way, I thought to myself, Timur and I might well turn out to be kindred spirits. We possessed the will to fight, perhaps, but could we live with killing another human being? It was an ability that many soldiers had discovered within themselves. No doubt some had found that they could shoot with ease, but many others would be scarred for the rest of their lives by what they had been ordered to do. For the first time since I picked up the sniper rifle, driven by rage, I dwelled on how it might change me. I was mindful of the fact that I had already been transformed by the loss of those I loved, but could I be responsible for breaking another mother's heart? Standing at the foot of that tree, I had no regrets about following my instinct here. It just remained to be seen whether I would find my true calling in this war.

From the lower boughs, Timur reached down and offered me his hand.

'I will find my own way,' I told him after a moment, blinking from my thoughts.

Much like a match that has flared, I could sense the anger and indignation within me begin to taper. What it left behind took me by surprise. Instead of the sense of darkness in which I had arrived on the front line, I found myself watching the boy make his way up the tree with a glimmer of pride at his courage and commitment. In the scramble to defend our soil, soldiers like Timur had been dispatched across the peninsula with little training or preparation. But I felt sorry for him as well. At his age, like my son, he should have been working in the fields with the sunshine on his shoulders. Instead, my boy was dead while Timur suddenly found himself struggling to free himself from the spur of a branch that had caught the shoulder of his tunic.

'Can you help me?' he called down, a little bashfully.

I chuckled to myself. In that moment, I knew that making my presence known to the boy back in the clearing had been the right thing to do.

'Of course.'

Carefully, I began to make my way up the tree. I had never attempted such a thing, only watched with anxiety many years before when my own child had first climbed this same trunk. I wondered what he'd make of me now. I even thought I heard him laughing at the sight. When I finally drew level with Timur, several minutes after my feet had left the ground, I found him hooked like a fish on a line. I smiled to myself behind my scarf, which must have been evident in my eyes because the boy smiled back at me. I asked him to turn around as best he could, and then clambered alongside.

'Do you think Zeki knew that he was going to die?' he asked, seemingly out of nowhere.

I took hold of the branch where it had caught his tunic. I was pleased that he had acknowledged me in this way; without demanding that I reveal my face in full or questioning what on earth I was doing here. We each had our reasons, and I hoped he recognised that was enough.

'Everyone dies in time,' I reminded him. 'All we can hope for is that it's quick.'

'And that we're not alone when our moment comes.'

Releasing the branch, I jerked my head clear as it swung towards me with a rush of air. As I looked back, the farmhouse caught my attention. Sometimes, my boy would call to me from up here in the trees and on hearing his voice I would step outside. It would always take me some time to spot him. Now I hoped I shared his skill at hiding.

'Surprise is on our side,' I told Timur. 'When they arrive we must use it to our advantage. I will shoot first, and you must be ready to follow it in a heartbeat. Is that clear? If they spot us, we will have nowhere to go.'

Timur nodded, seemingly relieved to be under instruction. Taking control like this felt quite natural to me. My husband and son were strong men, but in the farmhouse both relied on me for order and routine. I was keenly aware that feeding their bellies was a world away from firing a rifle. Despite my doubts, I would have to pull that trigger now, even if it changed me forever.

'You seem certain that they will come,' Timur said finally, and slapped at a midge that had settled on his wrist. 'How can you be sure?'

'Trust me. I know.'

Months earlier, when the officer paid a visit to the farmhouse and ordered me to leave, he explained that the ravine at the foot of the clearing was a point of vulnerability. Even with the coils of barbed wire hastily rolled into place, a determined detail could still creep through the scrub and get behind our lines. Zeki had lost his life within sight of the ravine, which told me the enemy had to be close at hand.

The sun was high overhead as Timur and I settled into the branches. It was hot and dry, but we were in shade. Every move we made caused the foliage to quiver. We kept as still as possible. Tucked under my thigh, my left foot lost all feeling, but I did not change position. In fact, when the tingling stopped and the numbness crept in, it felt as if I had begun to turn invisible. If I dared to look down, perhaps I would no longer see the boot borrowed from a dead soldier. There would simply be nothing there. And the longer I remained, the more of me would disappear.

For some time, to keep myself focused, I studied the rifle. The weapon was beautifully engineered, but hard to admire. My thoughts turned to the invading forces, and the campaign that they had mounted. The troops had poured from ship to shore in a show of strength that should have cowed us all. But it didn't. Now, in a position to join the fight, I had found the will to avenge the memory of the life I once had here. I just couldn't dismiss the doubt in my mind that this was the right way to do it.

'Are you frightened?'

The voice, just a whisper, drew me from the rifle sights.

We had been silent for several hours, and the question cut across my thoughts. I looked through the foliage. Timur was gazing up at me. A glimpse into his eyes told me he had been keeping his own counsel for too long.

'Put your fears into words,' I told him. 'It's the surest way to overcome all demons.'

Timur gazed out across the clearing. Some distance away, gunshot punctured the air. 'I'm scared that I'll never go home.'

Judging by the return fire, a fierce skirmish had erupted near the beach. This was how it had been for months. A kind of call and response that could break out at any point along the peninsula.

'We are Turks,' I said to remind him. 'This country is our home.'

My answer silenced him for a moment.

'So, what was life like for you?' he asked next, and gestured vaguely into the air. 'Before this.'

Weeds had sprung up around the farmhouse, I noticed. I felt a foolish urge to climb down and fetch the hoe from the store. Then I sighed at myself and shook my head. The place was history.

'Tell me about your family, Timur,' I said instead.

The boy faced up to me once more, squinting a little in the light. 'I miss my mother,' he said frankly. 'I told her I was old enough to fight. Now I feel I'm too young to be left out here without her.'

I wanted to climb down to him. Just to be close. It seemed

increasingly evident from such frank admissions that this was what the boy sought from me. I was only stopped by the thought that the swaying branches would give away our presence.

'Your mother will be proud of you,' I assured him. 'It's clear to me that you come from a loving home.'

'They say a good sniper should come from *nowhere*.' Timur grinned at me, wiping his cheek with the heel of his hand. 'Like a ghost.'

'Then let's be ghosts,' I said eventually. 'We come and then we go.'

It was then that the breaking of twigs across the clearing silenced our exchange.

Hurriedly, we return to our rifle scopes and scan the tree-line beyond the farmhouse. Timur whispers something at me. He sounds excited and scared in equal measure. I will him to be quiet. When the soldier creeps into my crosshair, crawling on his elbows through the long grass, I study him closely. It is the first time I have seen the enemy in the flesh. For months he has simply been an unseen force; a presence on the peninsula that I could hear spitting and raging, like a dragon from behind the ridge. My personal loss had made these men monsters in my mind, and yet the individual inching towards the farmhouse, tired and drawn, is nothing like I had imagined. He doesn't appear to be much older than Timur, with fear in his eyes and an uncertainty in his manner. For a second, I feel sympathy for him, and then shut the thought away. I have assumed the role of a sniper. I must live and breathe as one, or what hope do I have of making a difference in this war?

I hold the gun steady as the soldier progresses, and let him slip from my sights. Sure enough, another figure follows him out of the scrub; eyes bright against his muddy face, peering longingly at the farmhouse door. No doubt all food stores have been plundered, and with the roof destroyed the building provides little shelter. Even so, I understand what brings them closer. I only have to think about my own urge to come here. Without a doubt, there is something that reminds them of home in the ruins of mine.

I brace myself in case more figures appear. When it is clear that these two are operating as scouts, I find the first soldier in my sights once more. Between us, we can finish this within a matter of seconds. I slip my finger over the trigger, not thinking beyond the moment of firing, and that's when Timur's shot rings out across the clearing. I see the dust rise up an inch from the second soldier's head, and then a blur as the pair scramble to retreat.

'What have you done?' I hiss, for the boy has made a mess of our plan. With only two targets, we could have taken the soldiers out one after the other, as I had intended. Now, as they return fire from the undergrowth, yelling for support in that foreign tongue, we face real danger.

'I'm sorry!' he wails, and then gasps as a bullet tears through the branches above us.

With my heart kicking in my chest, I seek out the soldiers

in my rifle sights. A flash of fire marks the second shot. It hits the trunk beside me. Blindly I squeeze the trigger in response, hoping that I will find my target. In that moment, besieged by noise and panic, I can't even be sure that I have fired at all. As the soldiers reply, Timur's gasps turn to a shriek. I catch sight of him dropping his rifle, before he follows it down, a frozen expression on his face. He falls in a slow tumble, caught every few seconds by the branches of the tree, and then released again.

'No!' I cry, and scramble down the tree to be with him. 'No more!'

I give no consideration to my safety as I rush to reach the forest floor. I even miss my footing and fall the last few feet. Landing on my tailbone, the impact leaves me winded but no less determined to do something for the lost boy in a heap before me. My descent had been marked by the snap and whistle of yet more bullets, which promptly gives way to desperate shouting. I can only guess that I have escaped the soldiers' line of sight for now. Despite the voices, I clasp Timur's hand. He feels so heavy, as if gravity has suddenly conspired to bear down upon his body with brutal force. Blood trickles from his mouth and the wound in his chest. He rasps and gurgles, each intake of breath finding liquid in his lungs. But he does not take his eyes off me.

'Don't leave,' he mouths, his voice just a trace. 'Please.'

I tighten my grip. Another bullet strikes the tree behind us, followed by what sounds like a battle cry as the two soldiers seize the moment. It's then that I know, with absolute certainty, I have done the right thing in coming to the front line. Not to kill, as I had believed, but to comfort.

'You are not alone,' I promise the boy. 'I am here.'

The bullet, when it hits me between the shoulders, feels like a hammer strike.

I grasp at the throat of my tunic, which is hot and wet. Consumed by shock as much as pain, I am at the mercy of this final moment. Still clutching Timur's hand, as if it's my only purpose in this world, I slump across his chest. He grunts, choking briefly, and I feel his free hand flop across my back. There is no strength left as his palm lifts and falls, but when his fingers spread I succumb to his embrace.

'Mother,' he whispers, sounding elated and released from his fears, before his voice trails away along with my last breath.

Storm in a Teashop
by Mary Hooper

Storm in a Teashop

'Well, well, well,' said Grandad, rustling the 'War Latest' section of his newspaper.

Neither Mum nor I took any notice.

'Well, well, well,' he said again, and then delivered his punch line. 'Three holes in the ground.'

No one laughed. Well, you wouldn't, would you? Not if you'd heard it a hundred and one times before.

'Who'd have thought it,' he went on, prodding the newspaper. 'They're stopping folk having pigeons now! They're asking you to hand them over to the authorities. If you want to keep them, you have to have a special licence.'

'Why's that then?' I was forced to ask.

'Because, Harriet, the only pigeons allowed now are carrier pigeons – those flying about on war work.'

'That seems fair enough,' my mum said.

'Violation of our rights, that is! A man should always be allowed his pigeons.'

'You haven't got any pigeons,' my mum said. 'Never have.'

'I was going to get some,' said Grandad. We looked at him in surprise. 'Well, I was thinking about it.'

'You told me pigeons give you the heebie-jeebies,' Mum said.

'You said they've got nauseating habits,' I added.

'I can change me mind,' he said, turning to the next page.

We were six months into the War and Grandad was embracing it from every angle. He was too old to join up (though he'd tried, of course) and instead made a point of reading and reporting on its every aspect – especially any gossip and rumours. He'd put up posters in our front-room windows (YOUR COUNTRY NEEDS YOU! and WHAT DID *YOU* DO IN THE GREAT WAR, DADDY?) and would discuss battle tactics with anyone in the Dog and Duck who couldn't get away in time. I wouldn't have minded, but he had an opinion on every element and some of them were plain batty. Oh, and he'd also started a Give a Blanket to a Soldier campaign to encourage the locals to donate a blanket to our boys at the front. There was a pile just inside our door and I kept tripping over them.

I was concerned and apprehensive about the War, but as a girl there wasn't a lot I could do to help. I couldn't fight. At sixteen I wasn't old enough to train as a nurse or an ambulance driver, and I didn't want to work in a munitions factory, because the chemicals turned your hair and skin yellow. 'Wear the colour like a badge of honour,' they said about the factory work, but I wasn't having any of that. I didn't want frizzy yellow hair. I'd decided, instead, to get a job in London, a bus ride away, where there was lots more going on: rallies and parades, brass bands and marches. I thought I'd really get the *feel* of the war there, so I'd got a job as a waitress at the big Lyons' Corner House on the Strand.

The day before I was due to start work I went into my bedroom and put on the uniform: smart black dress with starched white collar and cuffs, little white hat and white apron. I tied the long straps in a bow around my waist and went downstairs to show Mum and Grandad.

'How's this?' I asked. I put on a classy accent. 'What would you care for from our bill of fare, modom?'

'Ooh, Harriet, you do look grand!' Mum said. 'Doesn't she, Dad?'

Grandad peered over the newspaper and nodded approval. 'You'll make a good waitress, lass. And it'll be first rate working up there in Charing Cross and seeing all our soldier boys coming and going.'

'That's what I thought,' I said, twirling round so they could see me from the back. The tea room was bang opposite the big mainline station, so I hoped to be able to dash over there sometimes and cheer the soldiers as they came and went. Perhaps some of them would pop in for a cup of tea, and I'd be able to wish them goodbye and good luck. If they were handsome, I might even offer to write to them. I knew it would be awfully worrying to have someone you loved actually on the front line, but it would be grand to knit him socks and send him parcels.

'The War Office is near where you're working – just up the road in Whitehall,' Grandad went on. 'That's where the generals get together to decide things like whether we can keep pigeons and how many potatoes we're allowed to have on our plates.'

Mum looked at me and rolled her eyes, and I went to change back into my ordinary clothes. I was already feeling quite nervous: I'd started worrying about getting people's orders wrong or dropping their macaroons on the floor.

Grandad was looking thoughtful as we sat down to tea. 'You know old Mrs Bertram in the corner shop?' he said. 'I think she might be a spy.'

Mum and I burst out laughing.

'You can laugh, but Dora says we've got to watch out for German spies.'

'Who's Dora when she's out?' Mum asked.

'D-O-R-A. Defence of the Realm Act,' said Grandad. 'DORA says we've got to watch for people infiltrating the system and pretending to be something they're not. In other words, *spies*.'

'Not old Mrs Bertram though!' I said.

'Bertram is a German-sounding name. 'Spect it's 'von Bertram' really. She's got a dachshund and I've heard her playing some sort of German music in the shop. Marching tunes and so on. What more proof do you need?'

'None of those things means she's a spy!' I protested.

'I'll tell you how you can find out,' Grandad said. Neither of us looked interested but he was going to tell us anyway. He lowered his voice to a whisper. 'Only spies know the second verse of "God Save the King".'

'*What?*' Mum and I said together.

He nodded. 'Everyone knows the reg'lar bit – 'happy and glorious' and all that – but who knows the rest?'

I shook my head, shrugging.

'Spies! That's who! Mince pies. People who aren't what they seem. People who feel they have to prove they're British by learning all the stations on the Metropolitan line off by heart or knowing the second verse of the National Anthem.'

'All right, Grandad,' I said. 'If I ever hear Mrs Bertram singing "God Save the King", I'll hang about and listen to her.'

'You can mock . . .' he said.

I felt very important travelling to work on the horse-bus the next day along with all the clerks, the businessmen in bowler hats, and the people in Army or Navy uniforms. One thing I noticed straight away was there were lots more women going out to work than there used to be. The bus conductor was a woman, for a start, and I saw a couple of lady lorry drivers and even a chimney sweep, poles balanced across her shoulder. People said it was a great time to be a woman, and that we would soon get the vote, but I wasn't sure I believed *that*. Mind you, everyone was pleased enough that we were doing the jobs that the men weren't around to do.

London looked much the same as usual but for the posters everywhere: SEND MARMITE TO YOUR MAN AT THE FRONT, they said; BREAD – THE NATURAL FOOD FOR THE TROOPS and JOIN THE ARMY AND HELP STOP AN AIR RAID!

When we went along Fulham Broadway I was amazed at the sight of a queue of men, maybe a couple of hundred of them, waiting patiently in line outside the Army Recruitment Office to sign up and fight. Burly, slight, tall, short, young, old; all waiting to do their best for their country. It made a girl feel proud, it did really.

The Lyons' Corner House I was working in was very smart: shiny black and silver, and almost as big as a proper department store. It had three different places to eat, and sold all sorts of foodstuffs, as well as flowers and chocolates. Ladies could have their nails painted or their hair done in the salon on the top floor.

I'd already done some training, so I was allowed to start in the ground-floor tearoom straight away. I was working under a supervisor called Milly Moffat, who'd been there for two years. Between us we had a nice little section right behind the front window – twelve tables each seating up to six people. The kitchens were at the back, so all we had to do was get people's orders and take them to the kitchen door where the manager would collect them.

Milly was twenty. She had her hair cut short in a bob, and had turned up her work dress and apron so that they were calf-length. 'It's so I can get about quicker,' she said, winking at me, but she knew and I knew that it was actually so the boys would be able to see some extra leg. 'I'll tell you this for nothing,' she said, 'the more you flirt, the more tips you get.'

'Really?' I said, and I pointed to the bottom of the bill of fare where it said, 'No gratuities allowed'.

'Stuff that,' she said. 'If you give good service, you get a tip. That's only right.'

'What if someone sees?'

She opened her eyes very wide. 'If one of my customers takes it into their head to leave me sixpence, what am I supposed to do? It'd be rude to refuse.'

'So you...'

'You just watch me, girlie.'

So that's what I did for a couple of days; followed her about like a puppy, seeing how she worked the tables. She flirted with the boys and complimented the girls – telling them she liked their shoes or their frock or their handbag – and if she served a couple she would teasingly tell them that she could see they were in love. Some customers left tips and some didn't, but she was nice to everyone.

After a week or so she trusted me enough to give me my own part of the floor and my own tables. We helped each other out if one was busy and the other wasn't, but apart from that she left me to my own devices.

As I'd hoped, we sometimes got soldiers in. Usually they were meeting up with the rest of their platoon over the road at Charing Cross, ready to leave Blighty later that day.

We made a special fuss of them, giving them extra-large portions and free top-ups of tea or cocoa. The pity of it was, we would only see these boys once before they caught their troop train to the coast, got on a ship and disappeared into the vast entity that was the War. There were a few boys I quite liked the look of, but I never got up the nerve to ask if they'd like me to write to them.

Apart from the boys in khaki, Milly and I both had our favourite customers – the ones we saw quite regularly who could be relied on for tips. I had two or three 'Specials', as we called them, and Milly had a very beautiful young lady she called Miss Clementine, because it sounded posh, though we hadn't got the slightest idea what her real name was.

Miss Clementine was in her late twenties, I should say, and terribly elegant. It was winter then and very cold, so she had a little fur hat with two pom-poms dangling from a ribbon tied under the chin. She wore a black astrakhan jacket and her skirts came down quite long, but swirled around her feet daintily, showing off her kid-leather ankle boots when she turned. She spoke in a throaty sort of voice as if she had a permanent cold and drew the eye of every man in the room. A couple of waiters even used to come from the big restaurant upstairs to ogle her from the doorway.

I'd only been at the Corner House three months or so when Milly announced she was leaving. She was going to be a VAD – a volunteer nurse – in a military hospital and, oh gosh, she did go on about it: how she was going to wear a natty uniform with a navy-blue cape lined in red, have a red cross on her cap and be chatted up by everyone: tommies, officers and doctors, too. If you were a nurse, she said, you were doing *real* war work, people applauded you in the street and let you into the cinema for nothing. They were desperate for nurses, apparently, because (rumour and Grandad had it) there were twice as many war casualties as they were admitting to in the newspapers. Milly made it sound so valuable and essential a job that I almost wished I was eighteen and could apply to be a nurse, too.

I missed Milly, but her leaving had its good side. The shop was short-staffed because of the number of waiters who'd got themselves war work, so until someone new arrived, I was going to be in charge of our little section on my own and would get to serve Miss Clementine. She would become *my* Special.

Grandad said, 'In my newspaper, it says we've got to keep the home fires burning.'

Mum and I looked at him. 'So?' I asked. 'What's wrong with that?'

'But how are we supposed to do it with no coal, no logs and no matches?'

'All those things have gone to the front!' I said.

'*Humph*...'

'That's what you want, isn't it: to help the tommies?'

'Besides,' Mum added, 'keeping the home fires burning doesn't mean literally. It means kind of – *spiritually*. Keeping faith.'

'How's spiritually going to help me chilblains?'

Miss Clementine nearly always had the same dinner: a rare roast-beef sandwich with horseradish sauce and lettuce, followed by a black coffee. So sophisticated! Sometimes, if she was in a hurry, she would eat one square of her sandwich and I would carefully put the rest of it in a greaseproof bag for her to take back to work. She worked as a personal assistant in a big fashion salon, she said, and sometimes, on my way home from work, I would walk down the Strand (also saving a penny on my bus fare) and look into all the shops in the hope of seeing her.

Miss Clementine talked to me like I was a woman, not a girl. She said I would break boys' hearts when I was older. She nearly always left a silver sixpence as a tip and was like the most glamorous, generous older sister a girl could ever want. She gave me a darling little bottle containing a smidgeon of perfume called 'L'heure Bleue' – she told me that meant the 'blue hour' – to use on special occasions. She bought me a brown velvet ribbon, which she said was a match for my eyes, and a bottle of nail varnish in Siren Scarlet. I wouldn't have dared put it on my fingernails – that would have meant instant dismissal – but I painted my toenails in this most startling, shiny red, so that when Grandad saw them he asked if I had a job as an exotic dancer. 'Girls today. . .' he said, shaking his head, but I just grinned at him. Times were changing, all right.

One day, about a month after Milly had gone, a man I'd

never seen before, tall and handsome as a movie star, came into the restaurant and sat at one of my tables. He was wearing a dark cashmere overcoat and a trilby hat. His coat bore a triangular brass badge, which meant he was in a reserved occupation and shouldn't be called out as a coward and presented with one of the dreaded white feathers.

I served him a Welsh rarebit and, afterwards, a cup of tea. When I took the tea over he was busy scribbling something on a paper serviette (upstairs, they had linen) and didn't look up. People should always be polite, I thought, so I said rather pointedly, 'Thank *you*, sir!' and immediately felt mean because he started, and said, 'Oh, I'm very sorry, my dear. Thank you so much. The rarebit was delicious.'

He drank his tea, still scribbling, then got up and went, leaving the serviette behind. I was just about to go over and clear his place when Miss Clementine rose from her usual seat and went past his empty table, waving to me on her way out. When I went over to clear the man's table, the serviette had disappeared.

'What d'you think I saw today?' Grandad asked that night.

Mum and I tried to guess, but couldn't.

'A lass, driving a big car!' he said. When we didn't react, he repeated, 'A *lass*, driving a *big car*!'

'And why not?' I asked.

'''T'aint natural, that's why not. It's like . . . like a rabbit riding a bicycle.'

Mum and I started laughing.

'But, Grandad, a woman working as a chauffeur or driver frees up a man to go and fight,' I said. 'That's a good thing, isn't it?'

He grunted. 'They'll be wanting to be doctors next, you mark my words.'

About a week later, a whole contingent of khaki-clad soldiers began forming up over the road on the station forecourt, all of them young and keen, laughing and joking. A hundred or more people had gathered to watch them, and some were pressing little presents of cigarettes and chocolate into the soldiers' pockets (they had a lot of pockets). I stood in the restaurant doorway, watching, and when they eventually slung their kitbags over their shoulders and marched off in formation to catch their train, everyone applauded.

'Did you see them?' I asked Miss Clementine, who came in just after they left. 'They looked all shiny and new.'

She shook her head. 'I'm afraid not.'

'No one in the crowd seemed to know where they were going. I wonder if...' My voice went wobbly and Miss Clementine looked at me enquiringly. Seeing a whole lot of soldiers like that – well, I couldn't help but ask myself how many of them would come back in one piece. I knew that some of the latest battles had resulted in terrible loss of life.

I pulled myself together. 'I do beg your pardon,' I said to her. 'Your usual sandwich?'

She nodded. 'Maybe with a little more horseradish.'

I ordered the sandwich from the kitchen and took it over to her, and then something a bit odd happened.

The handsome man in the cashmere coat had been in the restaurant again that day and eaten a slice of veal and ham pie. He paid his bill and went out of the door, leaving behind a brown envelope. I noticed it on the chair straight away and dashed over to get it, ready to run after him. But as I passed Miss Clementine's table, the envelope in my hand, she reached out to me and said, 'It's all right. I'll take that.'

'But he just left it. He's outside, I can—'

'He left it for me,' she said.

'Oh!'

She lowered her voice. 'You see, he and I are friends.'

'I didn't realise...' After all, as far as I could remember, they'd never even *looked* at each other.

'My dear girl, may I rely on your discretion?'

I nodded, breathless.

'We are more than friends. I trust you won't be too scandalised if I tell you we are lovers.'

'Oh!' I gasped again. How shocking... How wonderful!

'Unfortunately, we are both married to the wrong people, so at the moment all we can do is write to each other and try to express our feelings through poetry.'

'Oh, gosh. How awful for you. But how terribly romantic...'

She sighed deeply. 'My heart absolutely aches for him!' she said, tucking the envelope into her bag. Her hand squeezed mine. 'One day, my little chick, you will fall in love and then you'll know what it's like.'

I was probably gazing at her in a soppy way. 'Oh, yes, gosh, I hope so,' I managed to say.

'Of course, the angels are on the Allies' side in the War,' Grandad said.

'How d'you know that?' Mum asked.

'In the Battle of Mons,' Grandad said, 'angels appeared and fought on our side.'

'The angels had guns?' I said.

'Not guns,' he said irritably. 'They just appeared and . . . wafted about and helped us.'

'It's not true,' I said, remembering the story in the newspaper. 'It was invented. Just a story. The man who wrote it admitted he made it up.'

'No, he did not!' Grandad said furiously. 'You ask the boys who were there – they saw those angels all right. In long white dresses with haloes!'

I tried to make it easier for Miss Clementine and the Handsome Man. I moved his table slightly so that she and her rare roast-beef sandwich were in his direct line of sight, and made sure that any envelope either of them left was conveyed quickly to the other. He didn't come in every day, but when he did I saw them glancing at each other and could see the love reflected in their eyes – love, and a certain desperation, I thought. I longed to be in my twenties and as sophisticated and worldly as Miss Clementine. Imagine not only being married, but also having a lover!

One month went into the next and we heard that the War was escalating. Apparently, not enough boys were signing up to fuel the fighting, so the authorities were talking about bringing in conscription; that is, all single young men of eighteen or over would be made to go into the Army whether they wanted to or not. Everyone in the country had an opinion: some were for it, some against. Most of those who had already lost someone were very much against it, of course. Grandad changed his mind every day.

One day I was devastated to see the Handsome Man arrive at the restaurant with a woman; tall and pretty with fair, curly hair (though not a patch on Miss Clementine). They sat opposite each other and he ordered two slices of veal and ham pie. Was it his wife? I looked at her wedding finger – no ring. The cad – he was carrying on with two girls!

Feeling desperately sorry for Miss Clementine, I asked if she would like to move to a table behind one of the pillars, so she wouldn't have to see them together. She just smiled though, and said it was nothing at all to worry about; they probably worked at the same place.

But as I watched them, I began to feel that Miss Clementine was being bit gullible. The Handsome Man and the Other Woman were chatting in a very friendly way, and this seemed particularly cruel of him, seeing as he knew Miss Clementine was sitting just across the room. I decided, therefore, I would take my break as soon as they left, follow them and see if they really did work together.

Miss Clementine did not stay long that dinnertime, and there were no envelopes exchanged – which was hardly surprising. The Handsome Man asked for his bill (I was *very* frosty towards him), and when the relief waitress arrived from upstairs, I was ready to go after them.

I followed the pair across Trafalgar Square at a discrete distance, noting with pleasure that the woman was not holding the Handsome Man's arm. They went along Whitehall, talking all the way, then up Horse Guards Avenue, entering an imposing marble-faced building, set well back from the road. Once they had disappeared inside, I went closer and read the small brass sign on the gateway: War Office.

So they *were* work colleagues. And they were employed (just wait until I told Grandad) at the *War Office*. How very exciting!

As it was, I decided not to tell Grandad. I was tired of him banging on, and anyway, he was horribly old-fashioned about affairs and people taking lovers and all that. He'd be bound to think it was shocking, and that would take all the fun out of it.

The Other Woman (though, of course, she wasn't really this at all) did not come into the restaurant with the Handsome Man again, and things returned to normal, with envelopes going backwards and forwards, and Miss

Clementine and the Handsome Man giving each other swift, secret looks. I was dying to know if they ever met up properly, actually went out together, but I couldn't get up the nerve to ask Miss Clementine – and I'd never have dared to ask him.

About a week later, the Handsome Man came into the restaurant quite early, leaving a small oblong envelope on his chair. I collected it along with his empty plate and hid it, as usual, in my serving station, behind the stack of paper serviettes. I knew Miss Clementine would be in shortly for her sandwich.

But she didn't come.

I waited and waited – I didn't even take my dinner break – but by four o'clock, when we began serving afternoon teas, it was obvious that she wasn't going to turn up.

What should I do? After much thought, I decided to take the envelope home for safekeeping and bring it in the next day. If Miss Clementine didn't turn up again, I'd give it back to the Handsome Man as soon as he came in.

I don't quite know how the envelope came open but somehow, as a result of being jostled about in my handbag, the flap unstuck itself. Sitting on my bed at home, I debated with myself for a couple of moments and then curiosity got the better of me; I shook the envelope and let the contents drop out onto the bed.

It was a slim volume entitled *Byron's Selected Love Poems*, and I sighed when I saw it, for we'd done Byron at school and some of his poetry was very passionate. When, with a little encouragement, the booklet fell open, I saw that some words had been underlined, while others had scribbly writing next to them. The writing was pretty bad; I couldn't read a word – but then I realised that it wasn't written in English, but in a foreign language. How very strange. It didn't look like French. Could it possibly be...? No, I was getting as suspicious as Grandad.

I was about to put the book back into the envelope when a piece of paper fell out: a chart, by the look of it, written on very thin paper and folded over several times. I unfolded it: it was a list of names and dates in English. The names weren't those of people, however, but of battleships: HMS Dreadnought, Vincent, Collingwood, Neptune...I'd heard of most of them.

I stared at the chart. The dates were in the future. How curious. Were these the dates when the ships would put to sea, I wondered. But I knew – I'd read it in the papers – that the Navy never divulged information on when ships were going to sail for fear it should get into enemy hands. Somehow the Handsome Man had obtained this information and was passing it on to Miss Clementine. They must be...But no! I just couldn't believe it.

I had a sleepless night. Had I been the greenest, most gullible girl in the world – or was I simply reading too much into all this? Was I helping a sophisticated couple who had embarked on a love affair, or were they traitors, callously using me for their own ends?

I still didn't know the answer when, at eight thirty the following morning, I arrived at the War Office with the book of poetry and the chart. Was I doing the right thing? Or would they laugh me out of the place?

I had to wait in Reception until someone came to collect me. We went upstairs and into a little office where I told three nice men – one with a bristling military moustache – all about Miss Clementine and the Handsome Man, describing them in detail and adding that they were such polite and kindly people that there was probably nothing in it and the whole thing was ridiculous, and I was more than likely wasting their time. And they said, No, they were very pleased I'd gone along; what I'd handed in was *most* interesting and they'd definitely let me know if anything transpired.

And then I went to work and was only a little late.

I began to get really nervous near dinnertime, waiting for Miss Clementine or the Handsome Man to come in – and of course I'd left the poetry book and chart at the War Office so I knew I wouldn't have anything to pass on. I still had the empty envelope however.

Miss Clementine finally arrived at one o'clock, a little later than usual. I took her order and said it was nice to see her and I hoped she hadn't been unwell the day before. My voice kept going all funny: rushed and squeaky one minute, gruff the next. I just couldn't think how to be normal.

She shook her head. She seemed rather distant. 'I was much too busy yesterday to spare the time,' she said. She looked around the room; it was filling up quickly with the dinnertime trade. 'Was anything left for me?'

I nodded. 'I'll put in your order first, then I'll get it.'

'Could you be quick?' she said, quite abruptly, then added, 'In fact, I'll take my sandwich back to work with me.'

'Certainly,' I said – and you know that expression 'the scales fell from my eyes'? Well, suddenly the scales jolly well fell from mine. I was shocked both at the harshness in her voice and how different she seemed. She was no longer the generous, kindly older sister; there was a pursed tightness round her mouth, as if I irritated her, and she looked at me with hard blue eyes.

I gave her order at the kitchen and went to clear a couple of tables by the front door. Across the road at the station a military band had arrived and they were playing 'It's a Long Way to Tipperary' to the crowd who had gathered there. I heard someone calling, 'The troop train's in!' and, from all over the place, people started running towards the station forecourt.

I delivered two or three orders to my tables and then, forgetting my own little drama for the one happening over the road, I opened the front door of the tea room and stood there, watching. Most of the customers came too, including Miss Clementine, and as the band started on 'Pack Up Your Troubles', the injured troops began to limp through from the station.

They had come straight from the front line, I heard someone say, and it was heartbreaking to see them. Some were in wheelchairs or makeshift barrows; some on stretchers. Most of them, however, were 'walking wounded', limping along with the aid of a crutch or supported on each side by a mate. They winced with pain as they walked, trailed bloodied bandages behind them. Some were missing a limb; others blind. Some had iodine-stained cloth covering their heads and faces.

As more and more casualties poured out of the station, people began weeping, then applauding, patting the men on their backs and calling, 'Well done!' When the band got to the end of the song, it stopped. There was a pause and then it began, with much pomp and majesty, to play the National Anthem.

Everyone – the customers who had come out with me, Miss Clementine among them – stood to attention and joined in the singing with a passion. It was a spine-tingling moment and I felt my heart go out to the soldiers with their terrible injuries. These boys, this war, were what I should have been concentrating on, not some grubby love affair.

Moist-eyed, we sang the first verse, then the chorus, and after that everyone went quiet and blew their noses. Apart from Miss Clementine, that was. Her voice, clear as a bell, soared out over everyone else's:

'Oh Lord our God arise,
Scatter his enemies,
And make them fall!'

She got to the end of the verse and everyone clapped and cheered – then she saw me in the doorway and asked tersely, 'Do you have my letter?'

'Of course.' I passed her the envelope. She looked inside and saw – not a list of warships' names, but her roast-beef sandwich, rather squashed because it had been in my apron pocket.

'What on earth is this?' she exclaimed, but luckily I was saved from having to reply by the man immediately behind her – the one from the interview room, with the military moustache – putting one hand across her mouth and using the other to clamp her hands behind her back.

Two other men appeared and, one on each side, lifted her into the air and moved her towards a waiting black van. She struggled, kicked out and made noises, but luckily, in the hurly-burly of the crowd, and with people pressing to the front to cheer the injured soldiers, hardly anyone saw what was going on. A woman sitting inside the van jumped out and opened the back doors.

Just before she was shoved inside, Miss Clementine turned and gave me a look of pure hatred. I shrank back a bit, but then, as the injured tommies limped by, I took a deep breath, stood up tall and looked straight back at her, as brazen as could be.

A week later, I was both excited and terrified to be asked to go back to the War Office for what they called a 'debrief'.

This time it was just me and the moustachioed man. He stood up when I came into the interview room. 'I want to say that we in the War Office are extremely grateful to you,' he said, shaking my hand vigorously.

'So she really was...'

He nodded grimly. 'A German spy! Dropped over here with a false passport and false identity. Speaks damned good English, I'll give you that.'

'And what about the Hand— her boyfriend?'

'A traitor. Some blighter paid to betray his own country. Can you believe it?'

I shook my head.

He gave a tight smile. 'We've pulled him in, of course.'

There was still something puzzling me. 'But what about the poetry?' I asked. 'Where does Lord Byron come into it?'

'Oh, the book of poetry was a code-breaking device they sent backwards and forwards to each other. I'm very much afraid, Harriet, that they were using you as what we call a dead letter box.'

'Oh!'

'Thank God you realised.'

'Well, it took a while,' I said, slightly embarrassed.

'We're very, very grateful, of course,' said the man. 'If we could catch a few more...'

'I'll see what I can do,' I said.

I had to sign a form, something to do with DORA and the Official Secrets Act, to say that I wouldn't breathe a word to anyone. As I signed, I wondered what would happen to them – to Miss Clementine and the Handsome Man – but didn't want to ask. It wouldn't be anything good, that was for sure.

'I still can't believe it,' I said, shaking my head. 'She was so very *English*.'

'Spies are rather clever like that.' He stroked his moustache. 'Do you know, they say that only a spy knows all the words to—'

'I know what you're going to say!' I said.

And how very annoying that I wouldn't be able to tell Grandad.

The Marshalling of
Angélique's Geese

by Rowena House

The Marshalling of Angélique's Geese

While this story is fictional, it was inspired by real events, in particular by recent scientific discoveries about the origins of a deadly strain of bird flu known – misleadingly – as 'Spanish' influenza.

Summer 1916

I'm turning hay in the top meadow when I hear the squeak of rusty wheels and look up to see Monsieur Nicolas, the postman, peddling up the lane. I stiffen, suddenly afraid that I know the reason why he's here.

Please God, let it not be Pascal.

Soft summer sounds surround me now that I'm still. Grasshoppers. Distant birds. The eternal hum of bees. The creaking of the bicycle is like some infernal machine, let loose in the Garden of Eden.

Please God, not my brother Pascal.

I think about the day two years ago when the church bells chimed on and on. Pascal and I were stacking hay at the time. We dropped our pitchforks and ran to the village square, and heard the mayor announce: 'France is at war!'

Father went straight away. But Pascal stayed long enough to show me how to gather in the harvest, how to scythe and how to plough. I was twelve years old and so excited. Now I'm fourteen and my hands are calloused and my back aches like an old woman's.

Monsieur Nicolas clatters slowly past the orchard, waking the geese. They flap and hiss as they waddle towards the fence. Mother appears at the kitchen door, wiping her hands on her apron. Her back is very straight.

Monsieur Nicolas stops. He clambers awkwardly off the saddle and pushes his bicycle up the hill towards our gate. I hold my breath.

Please God, not Pascal.

He stops again and rests the bike against our fence. The geese clamour and shriek as he opens the gate. I pick up my skirts and run.

It is Father. 'Mort pour la France' and buried in some far-off field. Mother sheds silent tears as we close the curtains and change into mourning black.

I cry a little too, but in my heart I'm so relieved it isn't Pascal. I'm glad he'll run up the path some day and hug Mother and make her laugh, and tease me and demand to see King George, the finest pig in all of France, who deserves a name whatever Father says . . . whatever Father *said*.

I think about him as we walk to Mass that evening. I try

to remember something nice. But I can't. All I recall are his fists and his belt and his leather razor strop. Pascal got the worst of it but sometimes late at night I heard Mother whimpering as well.

Outside the church the other widows flock around Mother like crows.

Old Madame Malpas draws me aside, wringing her bony hands and crying, 'What's to become of you, Angélique? You'll very likely starve! La Mordue will go to rack and ruin without Monsieur Lacroix.'

'Pascal will be home soon,' I tell her. 'Mother and I can manage till then.'

'*Manage*, child? When your corn's still in the field in August?'

I glare at her. How can we start cutting corn when the hay's not stacked, and the cow needs milking, the geese need tending, King George needs feeding...?

'The farm-men have been promised leave,' I say. 'There'll be time enough to make a start when Pascal gets home.'

Madame Malpas sniffs. 'And you expect the generals to keep their promises? That'll be the day.'

I stick out my tongue as she stumps away. The trouble is she might be right. The farm-men were promised leave last summer too, but they couldn't be spared from the Front.

As Mother and I walk home through the warm, rosy dusk, a thought strikes me, a happy thought for once. The farm belongs to Pascal now. The house and land, King George and the geese, everything is his.

I hide a smile from Mother and make myself a promise. When Pascal comes home, he'll find the farm exactly the way he left it. I'll clean his tools and put them back in their proper places. I'll make his bed and lay his bowl and knife on the kitchen table. I think of it like a magic spell. If nothing changes – if I can make time stand still – then maybe Pascal won't change either and everything can go back to normal after this War is over.

No! It'll be better than before because Father won't be here.

Next morning I wake early and dress in the dark. The house is quiet. I hear the kitchen clock and the patter of rats in the rafters.

Outside, the cobbled yard is silver with dew. The air tastes clean and cool – until I go into the dung-heap warmth of the little stone barn which nestles against the house.

King George is snoring in his straw. The cow stands patient in her stall. I milk her, let out the hens, then fill a pail with grain for the geese.

There are twenty-seven Toulouse geese, big greyish-brown birds with dusky orange beaks. We call the gander Napoleon Bonaparte because he's so fierce. He hisses at me when I open the orchard gate, then waggles his head and cranes his neck until his beak is level with my chest. He could take out my eye with one peck – or so Pascal says.

Today is Friday, wash day, so after a crust and a cup of milk, I gather our dirty clothes and put them in a basket.

Mother's bedroom is empty. Friday is market day too. She has to leave at three a.m. to walk into town and back. I'm surprised she's gone today, though; I thought she might miss it for once.

Slipping into Pascal's room, I open his shutters. Dust tumbles in the sunlight. I take a musty shirt from his cupboard and a pair of breeches, and put them in my basket as well. Then I strap the basket to my back and walk into the village.

I like wash day. It's the only time I see my friends now that we've all left school. As I hurry across the square, I wave to my best friend, Béatrice Lamy, who's already standing at the big stone *lavoir* with her sleeves rolled up.

Madame Malpas is there too.

'Angélique,' she cries, 'have you heard the news? Monsieur Labrette and his youngest have both been killed at Verdun! Poor Madame Labrette has gone quite out of her mind.'

I make the sign of the cross, then put my basket next to Béatrice's and take out my scrubbing brush.

The gossip is all about the War. Monsieur Fournier's eldest is in hospital, blinded by mustard gas, and Pascal's friend, Henri Chevalier, is missing-in-action at the Somme. Monsieur Cousin, our old school teacher, has lost two nephews in one week.

Béatrice leans across to me and whispers, 'Do you think there'll be any boys left for us to marry?'

I go home deep in thought.

* * *

ROWENA HOUSE

When I arrive Mother is standing at the kitchen window, staring out. I wave as I open the gate, but she doesn't seem to see me.

That evening she hardly speaks. And the following morning, when I come downstairs, I find her sitting by the empty grate. She smiles at me sadly as I reach up for Pascal's bowl and lay him a place at the kitchen table. Then, silently, she walks away.

For the rest of the week I gather the hay by myself, and lead the cow along the verges to graze. In the cool of the evenings I sharpen Pascal's scythe or clean his boots. Then I lie in bed and listen to Mother weep.

I don't understand it. She can't have loved Father, not after what he did. I think maybe she's worried about Pascal but I don't know how to ask her.

Finally, one golden morning in early September, as I'm fetching down Pascal's bowl, Mother lays her hand on my arm.

'Put it away,' she says quietly. 'They aren't going to let him come home.'

'They might,' I reply.

'No, my angel, they won't.'

We sit in silence and eat a crust, then go to the cornfield together.

The ears of grain look grey. Some are mouldy. We scythe them down, slicing and twisting for hour after hour until my back is almost broken and sweat pours off my skin.

All the next day Mother rakes the corn into rows, while I

bend and stoop, bundling fat armfuls into sheaves. The brittle stems scratch my face and insects crawl up my sleeves.

On the third day we wake to a heavy stillness. We set to work straight away, but by ten o'clock the air is so hot it's difficult to breathe. We take off our caps and wipe our faces, glancing up anxiously. The sky is mottled grey and the sun pale and watery.

We work in a kind of frenzy now, praying that the storm will hold off, but by midday the clouds are low and solid. Thunder rumbles up the valley.

'That's enough, my angel,' Mother says. 'Stop now. We have to get the corn under cover.'

I nod. This is the moment I've dreaded. Before the War we had a horse and cart, but the army took them away, to pull their big guns into battle. So I am our pack animal now.

I bend over, bracing, as Mother ropes sheaves to my back. I stagger under their weight. Our threshing barn is only a few hundred metres away but it seems further with every load. As I run back past the orchard, Napoleon screams at me and young geese rush in panic along the fence. In the east, the sky darkens and crackles.

At last a fat raindrop strikes me, then another. Within seconds the storm is lashing my face and strapping my skirts to my legs. The geese splash and flap and screech.

Mother and I struggle on.

By dusk the field is a lake and the lane a torrent. Mud sucks off my boots, and I think if I fall I might drown.

* * *

Next morning every bit of me hurts. My shoulders, my back, my legs. As I lie rigid, staring at the ceiling, I wonder if I'll ever walk again or just hobble for the rest of my life.

Then I realise how selfish I'm being. What wouldn't Pascal give to be safe at home in bed? I rest for another moment, listening to a robin sing, and finally ease my feet to the floor.

Mother's room is empty. Of course, it's market day today. I sigh. Why must she always go? She never spends the money she makes from selling our butter and eggs.

Stiffly, I pick up her muddy skirt and put it in the laundry basket.

When I get back from the *lavoir*, smoke is drifting from the chimney. I decide Mother must be feeling better if she's lit the fire. But when I open the kitchen door I find her crouched over the flames, clutching a shawl around her shoulders.

'Mother! What's wrong?'

I run to her. She forces a smile.

'Nothing, my angel. It's just a chill from getting wet through yesterday. Don't worry about me. I'll be right as rain tomorrow.'

But she isn't. She's sweating and shaking so hard that she can't leave her bed.

'I'll fetch a doctor,' I say.

She grabs my hand. 'No, Angélique! We can't afford him.'

So I beg her to rest. I tell her I can manage. I promise her I can. I feed King George and the geese, milk the cow, churn butter, thresh corn, collect eggs, wash and cook and clean.

The next day is the same, and the next.

Every night I fall into bed, too exhausted even to dream.

Then, one damp afternoon in October, I'm up a ladder in the orchard, picking the last of the apples, when Napoleon shrieks underneath me and I drop my basket in fright.

Out in the lane there's a soldier, stroking his whiskers. His eyes glint from the shadow of his cap.

For an instant my heart leaps. Could it be Pascal?

No. He's a man, older than Father. He nods at me once, then wanders off as if out for a stroll.

I scramble down the ladder and run to the orchard gate. What if he's a deserter come to steal our food? I shoo the geese into the yard. No one breaks into our barns when Napoleon is roaming about.

That evening, when I bring Mother her supper in bed, she asks me why the geese are honking outside her window. I don't want to worry her so I say the orchard gate is broken.

But next wash day the gossip around the *lavoir* is all about the solitary soldier, and how he's been spying on the local farms.

Madame Malpas wrings her hands and says, 'I *knew* this would happen. Ever since my sister wrote to me, I just knew it would happen here too.'

'Knew what would happen?' Béatrice asks.

'You girls won't remember my sister Adèle, of course. She moved to Ariège thirty years ago and married that awful blacksmith...'

'Madame Malpas,' I break in. 'What about the *soldier*?'

'Well . . .' She glances over her shoulder, then lowers her voice. 'He's a scout, isn't he? For the army. It's the requisition.'

'The *requisition*?' Everyone around me gasps. 'But they've already been here! They took our horses and carts!'

'That won't stop them coming back,' Madame Malpas replies with a sniff. 'They'll be after food this time, cattle especially. Adèle said that in her village they came in trucks in the middle of the night and took every last cow. They hanged a farmer, too.'

'Why?' asks Béatrice, wide-eyed. 'What did he do?'

'He wouldn't let them take his cow. He only had the one. He told them, "Without that animal my family will starve."

'But the officer lost his temper. He said the men at the Front needed meat more than a bunch of selfish peasants. So the old boy lost his temper as well. He fetched out his hunting rifle and shot the officer dead.

'They hanged him at the next Assizes.'

I don't wait to finish my washing. I pack up my basket and run straight home to Mother. I want to hear her say that everything will be all right, that Madame Malpas is a foolish old woman who doesn't know anything.

But when I tumble into her room, she is sleeping peacefully for once.

I kneel by her bed, aching to take her hand and kiss it. Her cheeks are so thin I could weep. I watch her for the longest time, then creep downstairs, and into our gloomy little back room. I shudder, imagining I can still smell

Father's tobacco. Then I pull myself together and stride across to his desk – the one he bent me and Pascal over – and hunt through the drawers for ink, paper and a pen. Then I write a very long letter to my uncle in Étaples.

Days of waiting turn into weeks. I almost give up hope. What if my letter got lost? Étaples is hundreds of kilometres away. Or maybe Uncle Gustav won't realise that, while I don't say as much, in truth I am begging him to come.

Between my chores I watch the lane, keeping my fingers crossed.

Then, in November, King George falls sick. I blame myself for adding mouldy grain to his feed to make it go further. At first it upsets his stomach, but soon he stops eating altogether. I spend my evenings in the little stone barn, tempting him with titbits and mucking out his stall.

I don't mind, really. It's cosy in the flickering candlelight, with the cow quietly chewing the cud and the hens settled in the rafters like plump brown pillows.

That is where I am one windy night, with hail rattling on the roof and the candle guttering, when I hear the sound I've been expecting: Napoleon's sudden screech in the yard. My heart skips a beat. Is it my uncle or the soldier? I hardly dare open the door.

'Bloody bird! Call the damn thing off!'

'Uncle Gustav!'

I run to him. Hug him. I bury my face in his coat. He laughs and holds me close, stroking my hair.

'Oh, Uncle,' I sigh, 'I thought you weren't coming.'

'I'll always come, *ma petite*. But I had to find someone to help your Aunt Mathilde on our farm first. Didn't you get my letter?'

I shake my head. 'It never came.'

'Poor Angélique.' He smiles down at me, his dark eyes crinkling above his splendid white moustache. 'Come on, let's get inside, out of this weather. And if that ruddy bird pecks my backside one more time, I swear I'll put him in the pot!'

Mother scolds me at first for bothering Uncle Gustav with our troubles, but she can't hide the smile behind her tears.

'We'll soon put everything to rights,' he tells her. 'We can't have young Pascal coming home to a pickle, can we, *ma petite*?'

'No, Uncle Gustav,' I say. 'We can't.'

'Now, tell me what delicious thing you've prepared for our supper.'

'Er. Potato soup?'

'Perfect! And tomorrow it's my turn to cook. The only ingredient I'll need is your father's hunting gun.'

I find it for him next morning. He comes back from the woods with five pigeons, two rabbits and a duck. While he tends his bubbling stew, I light the lamps and build up the fire so it's warm enough for Mother to eat in the kitchen.

With each meal she grows a little stronger until, a fortnight later, she's back on her feet. I worry that Uncle Gustav will leave us now, but he seems happy enough, hunting and chopping wood and mending broken fences.

Late one evening, when Mother has gone to bed, he asks me to sit with him.

'Tell me, *ma petite*,' he says, 'why is your mother so anxious to go to market?'

'I don't know, Uncle Gustav, but she always went before she fell sick.'

'And have you been going for her while she's been poorly?'

'Well...' I sit up a little straighter. 'She never actually *asked* me to go. And it's such a long way and I've so many other things to do...'

He pats my hand. 'Of course you have, *ma petite*.'

Next Friday morning I feel guilty – but not surprised – to find Uncle Gustav's bed cold. I finish my chores, then pack up the laundry basket. Mother is sewing by the kitchen fire.

'Have a nice time,' she says, which makes me feel worse. I should have offered to go to market for her; I didn't have to see my friends every week.

I'm dragging my feet towards the village when I hear an unusual sound. A steady rhythm. Tramp. Tramp. Tramp. I stop and cock my head.

Tramp. Tramp. Tramp.

The sound gets louder, closer. I glimpse men in pale blue uniforms.

Dear God, no!

My hand flies to my mouth. I can't breathe. I'm rooted to the spot... Then I scream and drop my basket. I turn and run, leaping puddles or splashing through them. What does it matter? Except that now my skirts are heavier than lead.

Hitching them up, I race into the yard, shouting, 'Mother!'

Napoleon honks at me. I wave my arms to get him really riled up. He rushes about, his big webbed feet slapping against the cobbles. Mother appears at the door, her face pale and frightened.

'What is it, Angélique?'

'The requisition!'

She staggers against the doorframe. '*Mon Dieu!* What can we do?'

But I don't answer her. I tear into the little stone barn and haul the cow from her stall, pulling her into the yard and shoving her towards the back of the house.

'Move,' I plead as Napoleon pecks my legs.

Then, from the lane, I hear, '*Halt!*'

Napoleon knocks me over as he charges the gate, shrieking and beating his wings.

'Call the gander off or I'll shoot.' The man's voice is harder than iron. I whip round. Five soldiers are standing by the fence. One of them has braid on his collar. He shouts, 'One!'

'No!' I scrabble to my feet. 'Don't hurt him!'

'Two!'

I dash for the gate.

'Three!'

BANG!

'*Noooooo!*'

I lunge at Napoleon, flinging my body across his. Like a snake, he turns on me, slashing my face with his beak. I grab for his neck. Then I hear, 'Put the gun down, *madame*.'

Terrified, I roll over. Mother is pointing Father's gun at the sky. The barrel is smoking. I look back at the soldiers. They are lined up beside the fence, their rifles trained on her.

'*Put the gun down*,' I scream. 'Mother! Think of Pascal! You've got to be here for him!'

For a moment my universe hangs in the balance. The soldiers stand stock still. Mother could be a statue. Only Napoleon writhes underneath me. I need both hands to hold him down.

'*Please*, Mother,' I beg. 'Don't leave me alone.'

She drops the gun. Then, like a rag doll, she falls weeping to the ground.

We sit in the kitchen without speaking. Mother holds her head in her hands, crying silently, but I am too bitter for tears. I told the soldiers about Pascal being in the army and how Father died for France. But they wouldn't listen to me. They just led the cow away.

When Uncle Gustav gets back from market, I run to him and tell him all about it. He holds me very close, then kisses Mother on the forehead. But she won't be consoled.

'We've still got King George,' I tell her, trying to sound braver than I feel, 'and the geese and the hens.'

'And here...' Uncle Gustav empties a small bag on the table. It is the money he made from selling our butter and eggs. 'It's not much but it should help a little.'

Mother bursts into tears again. 'You don't understand. It's too late.'

Uncle Gustav and I exchange glances. She's more upset now than on the day when we learned that Father had died.

'What is it?' I ask her softly. '*Please* tell us what's wrong.'

Slowly, finally, sniffing all the while and wiping her eyes, Mother starts to talk. I can scarcely believe what I'm hearing. Father was a drunk and a gambler. He mortgaged the farm to pay off his debts and now, without the cow, she can't afford to pay the interest.

'Is that why you always went to market,' I ask her, 'and never spent the money?'

She nods. 'If I haven't made enough by next quarter day, the money-lender says he'll send in the bailiffs. They'll take the furniture first.'

I stretch across the table and take her hands in mine. 'We'll get by, Mother. We'll sell King George if we have to.'

She shakes her head. 'He's too weak to walk to market, my angel, and he's so thin we won't get much meat from him.'

'Then we'll just have to...' My eyes fly around the kitchen. What do we own that's valuable? Nothing much. Nothing at all, in truth. I take a deep breath. 'Then we'll just have to sell the geese.'

How could I say such a thing when Pascal loves those birds? He always has, ever since Father brought the first pair home from the goose fair in Monville. But what choice do we have? None that I can see.

But Mother shakes her head again. 'If we sell them now, my angel, we'll never get out of debt.'

'Why not? I don't understand.'

Uncle Gustav leans forward. 'Because, *ma petite*, with prices the way they are in Monville, you won't get enough for them to pay off the mortgage.'

'So?'

'So your mother has to pay back *everything* your father owed. Otherwise the money-lender will take every franc she earns in interest – and then come for the farm.'

I stare at him in disbelief, fear tightening my chest. I turn to Mother, then back to my uncle, my breath fast and short. 'But they can't do that, Uncle Gustav. It's Pascal's farm. Tell him, Mother. Tell him no one can take the farm.'

'I'm so sorry, my angel.'

'No! Stop it! I don't want to hear!'

My whole body is shaking. If only Pascal were here. Or Father, God help me. He'd never, ever give up the farm.

'Please, Uncle Gustav. There's got to be something we can do. I'll do *anything*, anything at all.'

'Well.' He scratches his ear. 'There is *one* possibility...'

We talk late into the evening. Uncle Gustav tells us about the War and how the soldiers near the Front are always hungry because there's not enough food to go around. He says prices have gone sky high in Étaples since the British army built their camp just over the railway track, and General Foch set up his headquarters in the nearby town of Frévent.

'If we leave right away, *ma petite*, we'll be there in time for the Christmas goose fairs. You'll be able to ask whatever you like for those fat, juicy birds of yours.'

I toss and turn all night, Uncle Gustav's words churning in my head. Where will I get the best price? Étaples or Frévent? Will I really be able to clear Father's debts? Is Mother well enough for me to leave her on her own?

It feels as if I've only just shut my eyes when, at dawn, she knocks on my door and comes in with a pair of Pascal's trousers, a shirt, a jacket and his stout walking boots.

'It's safer to travel as a boy,' she explains with a smile.

I dress in my brother's clothes. The material feels rough between my thighs, but it's thrilling to strut about without skirts dragging at my legs. Mother brushes my hair, then carefully tucks it under one of Pascal's hats. We go to her room so I can look in her mirror. I gasp when I see myself. It could be my brother staring back.

'Wear this too, my angel.' She takes off her silver cross and hangs it around my neck. 'And promise me, if you meet a ghost at a crossroads, you won't talk to it.'

Solemnly, I promise.

Downstairs, Uncle Gustav claps me on the shoulder. 'My word, Angélique! Don't you make a fine fellow? Have you made up your mind yet? Are we selling those birds to the British army at Étaples or the French soldiers in Frévent?'

'Why won't you tell me where to go, Uncle Gustav?'

'It's not my farm, *ma petite*. It's up to you and your mother to decide.'

'Mother?'

'Oh, I don't know, my angel. Your father always made these decisions.'

I take a moment before I speak. I feel very grown up but also small somehow. It's as if I'm on the edge of something great and once I've spoken there'll be no turning back.

I look about the kitchen one last time, at the objects I've known all my life and the chair where Pascal always sat. He'd want me to sell his geese to the French army, I'm sure of that. Then, all of a sudden, it occurs to me that General Foch might know where Pascal is.

Smiling at a secret hope, I turn around and say, 'Uncle Gustav! You and I are going to Frévent.'

We step out into a clear blue morning. Blackbirds sing. Icy puddles crunch underfoot. The geese pop up their heads in surprise when I open the gate to the lane.

My pockets are bulging with bread and cheese, and grain for the geese. I scatter a handful on the ground to tempt them to follow me.

A female ventures out first, stretching her neck and calling to the others. They waddle after her, talking softly back.

At the top of the lane I turn and wave. Mother is already a small figure in the distance.

Slowly, we climb past the fields and into the woods, me at the front, Uncle Gustav herding the stragglers from behind.

At midmorning we stop to rest. The geese graze and preen. There is a stream, and Napoleon goes in for a swim.

We continue on our journey.

At midday the sky clouds over. After lunch, Napoleon refuses to budge and we have to take a stick to him. His heavy body drags in the mud.

By mid-afternoon a clinging mist is closing in. We trudge through the murk, searching for the fork that will take us to the barn where we plan to spend the night.

'Are you sure we haven't passed it, *ma petite*?'

'I don't think so, Uncle Gustav.'

A yellow pinprick of light punctures the gloom. We approach it cautiously and find an old woman bent over an open fire, roasting a rabbit on a spit. Her cart is parked on a narrow crossing track, and her scabby horse is tethered to a hawthorn tree.

'Good evening, *madame*,' says Uncle Gustav.

The woman does not look up.

'A dirty night,' he adds.

Still she tends the charred remains of her rabbit.

'We're going to the railway station at Monville,' I say. 'Are we on the right road, do you know?'

Uncle Gustav sucks his teeth and the old woman looks up sharply. I step back, afraid.

She doesn't have eyes. Just empty, withered sockets.

'Tell your fortune, my angel?' Her voice is thin and wheezy.

'How do you know my name?' I demand.

'It's written in the stars.'

Rolling his eyes, Uncle Gustav pulls me away. 'Good night, *madame*, and *bon appétit*.'

Night falls. The fog lifts. We're on an open heath which I don't recognise, but soon there is moonlight enough to know for certain we're lost.

'Look,' says Uncle Gustav, pointing to a windmill, high on a ridge. 'That'll have to do for tonight.'

The breeze picks up as we cross the heath, weaving between tussocks and mires. As we draw near, I hear the windmill's sail-arms creak and the door banging on its hinges.

The geese refuse to go in.

'They'll be fine outside, *ma petite*.'

We climb a rickety ladder and make mattresses out of old, floury sacks. The place stinks of rats. I lie in the freezing dark, listening for their claws, afraid they'll eat my face in the night and I'll be too numb with cold to notice.

In the early hours I wake to find Uncle Gustav gone. I hurry down the ladder. Outside the silence is profound. The wind has died and frost shrouds the ground. Above me, the ice-ringed moon peers down like an eye.

'Careful you don't catch your death, *ma petite*.'

Startled, I jump as Uncle Gustav emerges from the shadow of the mill. I run into his arms. Beyond him, the geese stand staring at the sky, a forest of necks and gaping beaks. Following their gaze, I see skeins of flying birds, wave upon wave of them, like endless flights of arrows.

'What are they?' I ask.

'Wild geese from the north.'

'What are they doing this far south?'

'There must be a cold winter coming.'

He holds me close as we watch them. I've never seen such a sight. Our geese grow restless. They call and flap. Napoleon spreads his wings as wide as he can reach. My heart bleeds for him. I wish he could take off – just once – and wheel free in the glittering heavens. But he's too big for that; his feet can't ever leave the ground.

As if he knows it, he lets out a mournful cry. The other geese join in and from far away I hear an eerie whistle. The wild geese are calling back.

Then one phalanx breaks off and circles the moon. They fly low towards us. More birds break ranks, then more and more, until an almighty host swirls about us, their dark bodies seething across the heath. Our geese vanish as if beneath a sea.

Amazed, I ask, 'Have they come to take our geese away?'

Uncle Gustav laughs. 'No, *ma petite*. They're only visiting.'

He's right. The wild geese are gone by dawn. In the grey light, the land looks empty without them. Our geese feed and preen as if nothing has happened. I watch them for a while, glad they can't understand where I'm taking them – and that they won't be coming back.

Not that all the wild geese have come safely through the night. As we retrace our steps back to the road, we find dozens of bodies lying among the tussocks or floating in the mires. I stop and admire their sculpted black feathers.

'Don't touch them, *ma petite*. We don't know what they died from.'

'Isn't it just the cold, Uncle Gustav?'

'Perhaps. But I wouldn't expect to see so many of them dead. These birds are used to the cold.'

I nod but say nothing more.

At the road we turn north, guided by the low winter sun. The geese walk more slowly today. It takes us hours to herd them off the heath and into familiar valleys again.

As soon as I know the way, we chivvy them along, past fields and farms. Another hill. Another valley. We rest them as briefly as we can.

Just after three I spy the rooftops of Monville, faint like sketches in the mist. We stop by the roadside one final time. The geese paddle in ditches, then ruffle their feathers and settle, all the while holding their secret conversations.

There are other people on the road, driving sheep or herding ducks. One girl about my age is grazing two cows on the verge. Two! I feel a stab of jealousy.

Then, in the distance, I hear an unfamiliar hammering

sound. Everyone turns to look, and although we can't see anything, the noise grows steadily louder. Uncle Gustav climbs on a wall. Then he mutters, 'Damn it.'

'What is it, Uncle Gustav?'

'It looks like an army truck to me.'

No! It can't be. Not again. A knot tightens in my stomach. 'Are you sure?'

But by now even I can tell it's the noise of a motor vehicle.

The lane empties. I see the girl drag her cows behind a hedge and a man stuff two chickens under his coat. But our geese are scattered; there's no time to hide them.

'Quick! Angélique! Over here!'

Uncle Gustav pulls me behind a tree and we squat together in the damp grass. I shut my eyes and pray. *Please, God, let them pass us by.*

The hammering is inside my head now and I fancy I smell engine oil. I try my hardest to stay hidden, but in the end I can't help it. I steal a peek up the road.

A sludge-green lorry with a flapping canvas top is coming towards us, pitching and wallowing like a runaway cart. Two men sit in the open cab: a driver with a thick moustache and a passenger in a braided cap. An officer, I guess. They both stare straight ahead until . . .

I dip my head, desperately hoping they didn't catch my eye. I pray they're going too fast to stop. Or that their brakes are rotten and they'll crash into the ditch. But God isn't listening. With a squeal of tyres, they skid to a halt. There's no one in the road except them and us.

Uncle Gustav stands up, legs apart, hands on hips. Napoleon flaps and hisses. The driver and the officer climb out.

'*Monsieur*,' says the officer.

'*Monsieur*,' says Uncle Gustav.

Neither man touches his cap.

'Hmm,' says the officer, turning to me. 'Off to market, are you, lad?'

Heart thumping, I stare at my feet.

'Speak when you're spoken to,' orders the driver. 'And afterwards you and me will have a little chat about what a strapping young chap like yourself is doing shirking his patriotic duty.'

Uncle Gustav bristles. 'That is my niece you're talking to.'

'Ah,' says the officer, smiling. 'So you're helping your uncle take his geese to market, are you, *mademoiselle*?'

'No,' I say as stoutly as I can. 'The geese don't belong to him.'

'So *mademoiselle* can speak.'

'Yes I can! And I've a right to be heard!'

'Hush, *ma petite*. The gentleman was only teasing.'

Teasing? *Teasing!* When I'm being forced to sell Pascal's geese? I'll give him teasing! I stand up straight, square my shoulders and look him in the eye.

'These geese belong to my brother, *monsieur*, who's a soldier just like you. So don't think you can take them – because you can't. *I* won't let you. Me! Angélique Lacroix. These geese are going to General Foch himself. And yes, I'm selling them, not giving them away, because I need the money to save my brother's farm. That is *my* duty, *monsieur*, and I'll not let anyone stand in my way!'

The officer's eyes are out on stalks. His jaw is hanging open. Have I gone too far? Will he hit me like Father would? Will he lash me till I bleed? My heart races and my cheeks burn until ... He throws back his head and *laughs*.

'Well said, *mademoiselle*!'

With a flourish, he pulls a notebook out of his pocket and writes something down. Then he tears off the piece of paper and hands it to Uncle Gustav.

'*Monsieur*.' The officer bows. '*Mademoiselle*.'

He tips his cap to me, turns on his heels and jumps into the cab. The driver hurries after him and they're gone, disappearing in a farting cloud of fug.

Speechless, I look at Uncle Gustav. He's staring at the piece of paper, his mouth moving slowly.

'What does it say?' I ask him.

He sits down heavily.

There are tears in his eyes. He rakes his fingers through his hair.

'Uncle Gustav! What does it say?'

I snatch the paper from him. It's covered in fancy scrolls and headed with ornate printed words: 'Liberty. Equality. Fraternity.'

'But this is terrible,' I cry. 'It's an official requisition form!'

'Read what he wrote, *ma petite*.'

Slowly I spell out the letters. It's difficult because the writing is large and flowery, but in the end I work out what it says.

Gaping, I read it again:

By Order of the Government of France, the Geese in Possession of Mademoiselle A. Lacroix Are In Transit to His Excellency General Ferdinand Foch. Priority Passage Requested.

Uncle Gustav starts to laugh. So do I. He leaps up and punches the air. I dance a jig in the middle of the road. He grabs my hands and we're twirling, twirling, and Napoleon is honking and the world is such a wonderful place to be.

'They can't stop us now, Uncle Gustav! No one can stop us now!'

We march into Monville in triumph. Street lamps shine. Shop windows sparkle. We ignore the dingy back streets and swing along a wide boulevard.

At the railway station, there's a glorious kerfuffle. We wave our official paper. The station master waves his arms. There's no time to waste because the train to Paris is already approaching the platform. A black smoking monster of a train. The screech of its wheels is deafening.

The geese panic. It's all I can do to stop them from plunging onto the tracks. I run after them, followed by Uncle

Gustav, the station master, a handful of passengers, the guard from the train. We rush along the platform, grabbing the geese, and carry them, squawking, into a cattle truck.

The guard slams the door behind us, and Uncle Gustav and I burst out laughing again. Exhausted and in pitch darkness, we're on the next stage of our journey.

I've never been so cold in my life, not even last night in the windmill. As we hurtle along, blades of ice slice through the wooden slats. I can't escape them no matter where I sit.

And the noise! The horrible clanking clatter that batters my ears all night long. Heaven knows how Uncle Gustav sleeps through it.

Now and then I hear the train whistle and we slow to a halt. The guard calls out the name of a town, but it's never, ever Paris.

At last dirty ribbons of daylight fall across the floor and I touch Uncle Gustav on the shoulder. He opens his eyes and smiles up at me.

'Did you get some rest, *ma petite*? We must be nearly there.'

But the day crawls slowly past. We idle in stations, seemingly for no reason, and stop in lonely sidings, waiting for other trains to overtake. The afternoon is fading before I see tall buildings through the slats. Warehouses. Chimneys. The Eiffel Tower!

'Uncle Gustav,' I shout. 'We're here!'

'So we are, *ma petite*.'

For a few minutes more the train clunks on. Then, with a wheeze, we stop.

Uncle Gustav slides open the door. We're in a smoke-filled cathedral of iron. The air reeks of soot and there's a distant roar like the wind in trees. I jump down opposite a sign saying Gare d'Orléans. The platform seems longer than the lane to our farm.

We coax the geese off the train, then lure them along the platform with a scattering of grain. At the gate to the concourse they stop, huddling together, hissing and waggling their heads like the picture of the Gorgon I once saw in a book.

And who can blame them? There are hundreds of people out there – men, women, children, porters and beggars – all bustling about.

'Here, *ma petite*. This might help.'

Uncle Gustav gives me a piece of string. I tie it round the neck of a young female and gently pull her forward. The rest of the flock stays close with Uncle Gustav shooing them from behind.

The streets outside are just as busy. All of Paris seems in a rush. I see gas lamps. A bridge. Chestnut stalls. Milliners' shops. The smell of fresh bread makes my mouth water.

At the Place de la République, Uncle Gustav buys us baked potatoes, hot off a brazier. I cup mine in my hands to thaw out my fingers, and watch the geese splash happily in a fountain. Their antics draw a crowd: soldiers in uniform and ladies in feathered hats. A group of small boys starts to laugh.

At first I laugh with them, but then I see what they're up to. A little goose is stuck in the fountain. She's flapping and frightened but the boys won't let her out.

Angry, I chase them away and lift the poor bird onto the pavement. She's too tired to walk so I tuck her under my jacket as we set off again.

The Gare du Nord is a sombre place, full of men in different coloured uniforms. Some have different coloured skins.

'Where do they all come from?' I whisper to Uncle Gustav.

'The four corners of the earth, *ma petite*.'

He disappears into the ticket office and I wait with the geese under the station clock.

Train after train disgorges its cargo of men. Officers step out of carriages, while the ordinary soldiers jump down from trucks. Do any of them know Pascal, I wonder. Could one of them be him? I pass the time by studying their faces.

The clock is striking ten p.m. when Uncle Gustav returns, walking behind a stout railway official in gold-rimmed spectacles. The official counts the geese twice, then writes 'twenty-seven' in his big red ledger and snaps it shut.

'There!' He thrusts our piece of paper into Uncle Gustav's hand. 'Now be off with you. I have paying passengers to attend to.'

Uncle Gustav bows. 'Thank you, *monsieur*. I'll give your respects to General Foch.'

Scowling, the official stomps off.

'What was that all about?' I ask.

'Let's just say he's not too fond of letting geese travel for free.'

There are only soldiers waiting by our next train: grim-faced men with bed-rolls and backpacks and boxes strapped to their belts. Some carry rifles. A few of them are singing. The smoke from their cigarettes mingles with the smog.

Glancing back, I see the stout official talking to an officer. They look in our direction, and the official points at us.

'Uncle Gustav.' I tug at his sleeve.

'Uh-oh. What's up now?'

The officer is walking towards us, waving his stick.

'Let me handle this, all right, *ma petite*?'

I feel a flutter in my stomach. Is something wrong? Will we be allowed on the train? I find myself holding my breath.

'*Monsieur*,' the officer calls. 'You have supplies for General Foch?'

'Yes, *monsieur*,' replies Uncle Gustav. 'Is there a problem?'

'There is if you expect to find him at Frévent.'

Uncle Gustav stiffens. 'But I've seen his camp for myself.'

'If you did, *monsieur*, you should keep it to yourself. Military locations are not a matter for public discussion.' The officer flicks his eyes at me. 'That goes for you too, lad. Not a word. Paris is a nest of spies.'

He turns to Uncle Gustav again. 'You have a requisition chit?'

Uncle Gustav hands over our piece of paper. Frowning, the officer reads it.

'And who is Mademoiselle Lacroix?'

I step forward. He raises an eyebrow but only says, 'And these geese belong to you?'

'No, *monsieur*, they belong to my brother, Pascal Lacroix, but he's at the Front. I was hoping General Foch might know where he is and that perhaps he might let me see him.'

'Why?'

Blushing, I look down. 'I . . . I . . .'

'Speak up, *mademoiselle*. What is it?'

'I want to give him a goose for his Christmas dinner.'

The officer sighs deeply. He looks me up and down, shaking his head, but then his expression softens a little. 'By rights I shouldn't tell you this, so don't go spreading it around. But there's no point in looking for your brother at Frévent – or any of our lads for that matter. General Foch has been pulled back by the High Command because people are saying it's his fault we lost so many men at the Somme. Utter nonsense if you ask me, but there you are. People have to blame someone for this abominable War.'

He turns to Uncle Gustav. 'Where were you going after Frévent, *monsieur*?'

'Étaples.'

'Indeed?'

'It is my home town.'

'I see.'

Suddenly, the train lurches backwards, shunted by a belching locomotive. The platform billows with smoke and grit. I see the railway official vanish in a cloud of soot. The officer folds our piece of paper and gives it back to Uncle Gustav.

'In that case, *monsieur,*' he says, 'I'm sure you know another camp where they'll be glad of a Christmas goose. I hear the food there's atrocious.'

He touches his cap and marches briskly away.

'Come on, *ma petite*. Hurry up. This is still our train.'

'But where are we going?' I ask as we load the geese onto the nearest cattle truck and clamber up behind them.

'To sell your geese to the British soldiers at Étaples. Their money is just as good as General Foch's.'

'I know it is, Uncle Gustav. But we won't find Pascal there, will we?'

Sadly, he shakes his head. 'No, *ma petite*, we won't. But we will find a lot of other very brave boys. English, Irish, Scots, Canadians, Australians, New Zealanders, Indians. Half the British Empire is there. All packed in together, the wounded and the sick as well as the fighting men. They say,' he adds quietly as we shut the geese into pens, 'that the training inside the camp is so brutal that some of them are glad to get to the Front.'

Shocked, I stare at the young men who are throwing their kit into our truck and climbing up after it. Are they British, I wonder. I don't think so. But how could I tell? They just look like soldiers to me.

Close up, I notice something strange in their eyes. A kind of blindness as if they can't see the filthy wagon we're in, only things far away. Is that how Pascal looks? Is that what this War has done to him?

Sighing, I kneel by the little goose who got herself stuck in the fountain. She's lying on her side, blinking up at me. I pick her up and feel her flop against my arm.

'I think she's sick, Uncle Gustav.'

'Ah, well. Keep her apart from the others, then.'

I lay her in my lap as we wait for the train to leave. More and more soldiers scramble aboard until we're jammed together like meat on a butcher's cart.

When at last we move off, my eyes shut of their own accord. I fall asleep praying that tomorrow we will reach our journey's end.

'Abbeville! Abbeville! All change at Abbeville!'

The voice of the station guard seems to come from the depths of a well. Or perhaps it is me who is in a dark hole where the air is so cold that my lungs have turned to ice.

'*Ma petite?*' Uncle Gustav shakes my arm.

I don't want to wake. I don't want to remember where we are or where we're going, or endure the pain of forcing my frozen limbs to work again.

'We have to change trains, *ma petite*.'

I open my eyes. The wagon is still, the door open. Outside in the darkness I see lanterns and men and mules. Their breath smokes just like the trains.

Standing up is slow agony.

'Where's my little goose?' I ask.

Uncle Gustav squeezes my hand. 'It was for the best, *ma petite*. She was suffering.'

Tears spring to my eyes. I try to hide them because I know it's wrong to cry for a goose when so many men are going to war. But truly I can't help it. I stroke each bird as I pass them out to Uncle Gustav. Napoleon hisses at me but I risk a quick pat anyway.

On the platform I count them. Then count again. I can't bear to ask why there are only twenty-four.

Around me, the soldiers look sullen or sad, or still afflicted by that strange blankness I saw at the Gare du Nord. Just once I hear a ragged cheer as a train grinds through the station, shaking the platform with the weight of its load. Standing on tiptoe, I see that one of the wagons is a solid black shape: a colossal cannon with a gigantic barrel pointing into the night.

'Look, *ma petite*. They call those the Devil's Gun.'

'I see it, Uncle Gustav.'

But I don't feel like cheering.

Our train arrives. Horses are led aboard. We share a wagon with soldiers and chickens, even a pig. We set off slowly, crawling through flat countryside.

A young soldier slides open the door. I stand next to him, looking out. The air is tainted with soot but I'm used to that now. I watch silver pools slipping by and the wild marsh grasses rippling.

I have a sudden impulse to set the geese free. If they could fly, I really think I might. The farm feels so far away that saving it seems less important somehow. But I summon up a picture of Mother and Pascal together again, and step back from the door.

At last we clank into a siding and stop. Everything goes quiet. The vast, icy stillness of the night enters the wagon. The geese lift their heads. Can they sense the water, I wonder, and the wilderness?

I'm surprised when Uncle Gustav takes my hand and says, 'Don't be afraid, *ma petite*. Sound carries a long way at night.'

I'm about to ask him what he means when lightning flickers in the east. It flashes distantly again and again. Minutes later I hear the first thud of thunder.

Except that it isn't thunder. Or lightning. I can tell from the pain in Uncle Gustav's eyes.

'Is that the Front?' I whisper.

He nods. 'Artillery. You can feel the vibrations when they fire the really big guns.'

Horrified, I watch and listen. Are those our shells raining down or theirs? Does it matter? The suffering underneath must be just as great.

Soldiers climb out of their wagons and stand by the tracks. I join them, despite the biting cold which freezes my tears to my face. Quietly, Uncle Gustav lays another limp goose on the ground.

I don't know how long we stay there, how many hours the sky glimmers and the dreadful rumbles roll across the land. Outside I'm numb. Inside I burn with pity for

Pascal. For the men who stand beside me. For the living and the dead. Even Father. How can the world ever be the same again?

At last a bugle sounds and the soldiers move as if waking from a trance. Uncle Gustav and I climb aboard too, and the train heaves forward. We enter Étaples at dawn. In silence.

Scientists now believe that the presence of live geese, ducks and chickens – plus horses and pigs – at the infantry and hospital camp at Étaples created a breeding ground for a deadly avian flu virus which became known as 'Spanish' influenza. The first cases were recorded during the bitter winter of 1916–17. At the end of the War, soldiers returning home via the camp spread the disease around the world, causing a global pandemic which killed at least fifty million people.

Mother and Mrs Everington

by Melvin Burgess

Mother and Mrs Everington

Mother was busy knitting. I think that she must have knitted over a mile of scarves and enough socks to clothe the feet of nations. She had the maid and the cook doing the same and tried to get me at it too, but I told her I'd rather stab my eyes out than sit still knitting all day when our young men were dying for their country.

'What are the troops going to do with all these scarves, Mother, strangle the Bosch to death with them?' I asked.

'It's all about morale, Effie,' she said. 'It shows the men that the women are behind them.'

Behind them, indeed! What Mother doesn't realise is that this War, dreadful though it is, is a wonderful opportunity for us women to show the men what we're made of. Women of her generation may be used to being things of ornament, panting their lives out in a whalebone cage, but that's not for me. I want to be an inspiration. And if I can't be that, I'll damned well be useful at least!

Sorry for the language. As you can see, I feel strongly about it.

So while Mother and her dear fat friend Mrs Everington were producing scarves by the mile, I was learning how to drive. I commandeered my brother Robbie's little car and drove it round and round the paddock behind the house, churning up the mud and scaring the pony half to death. I got Jimmy, the milkman's boy, to teach me the basics. He was scared to come with me at first, but within a few hours I could drive better than him. That's what he said, anyway, although as soon as he was out of the car he claimed it was just an excuse to escape.

'You're a wet blanket,' I told him. 'If you're scared of me driving you around a field, how are you going to cope in the trenches? Or is that why you haven't joined up yet?'

Jimmy said he'd rather face the Bosch than my driving any day. 'And I'm not eighteen yet, miss,' he said. 'It'll be another year and more before I'm old enough to fight.'

'That didn't stop my brother, did it?' I said. Robbie did the bravest thing and lied about his age in order to fight for his country. Mother helped him – it's amazing what you can get away with if you're only born a male. She wrote a letter assuring the draft that he was over eighteen, and ready to go. Mrs Everington was furious about it and told her she was putting the men at risk, sending a boy out to do a man's job, but we all know she was just jealous. Her son Howard joined up at eighteen and she was livid that Mother had stolen a march on her. You should have seen her face when she heard! If she'd had a genie in a lamp, I swear she'd have got him to conjure her up another son, a month or so younger than Robbie, just to win back the edge.

It's pathetic, really, but Mother is just as bad. They are at it hammer and tongs, desperate to outdo each other in the War effort. Still, it was a triumph for us, no denying it – and you should have seen the party we put on when Robbie left. Mother made a cake iced in the Union flag and I painted a scene in watercolours of the trenches with our brave boys chasing the Hun across Flanders mud, and nursing their noble wounds back in the trenches.

I think I shamed Jimmy in the paddock that day, but he would have been horrified if he'd known what I was planning. It's no use us women crying out for the vote and equality all warm and dry in our cosy sitting rooms while the men are out there sacrificing their very lives for King and country. We have to show them that we are their equals. In fact, we have to do better than them, be braver and more willing to risk everything, even though we're weaker in body, if we're to win back those centuries of lost pride. And Mother and Mrs Everington are content to knit while the menfolk give all!

Not this generation – not this woman! I told Robbie I was going to drive the butcher's van so as to give a fit young man a chance to go to the Front, but that was never my real idea. I wanted to be where the action was. I had set my heart on being an ambulance driver.

I was ready to find my way to the Front that very week but I had to put it off because – great news! – Robbie was on his way back to us! He had been wounded – nothing serious, thank God, just a bullet through the leg, but they'd sent him home to the loving arms of his family, to get better the faster so he can return to fight the Hun.

Of course, we went to town all over again. Mother invited Mrs Everington over to join in the festivities. She came, although she was clearly livid that our family had been the first to shed blood for our country. We were so proud! We got out the bunting and put Union flags out of all the windows, and red, white and blue flowers on every surface. Father took time off from his work in town, which he hardly ever does during these days of National Emergency.

Father and Mother went to pick Robbie up from the station, but I had something else up my sleeve. I wanted to give him a surprise, you see. I was hidden behind the curtains in the sitting room ready to jump out on him, like we used to only a few years ago – gosh, it feels like an age! – when we were still small. The trick was that even though the other might guess you were hiding, you still had to catch them out and make them jump.

If I had only known the unknowable – the unthinkable! What can I say? The whole thing went disastrously wrong.

I waited until they were all gathered in the sitting room. I was certain Robbie must know where I was. It was just a game, that's all. I waited until he was settled in the armchair by the standard lamp, with everyone around him talking admiringly about how smart he looked in his uniform. Then I leaped out with a terrific yell.

It was terrible. I never regretted anything so much in my life. Robbie jumped to his feet with a terrible roar.

'Effie, you stupid bloody cow,' he bawled. His whole face twisted with rage. I swear for a moment he looked like an angry dog. The whole room froze. It was the worst moment of my life.

'Watch your language, sir!' Father snapped at him. And Robbie – God help us, poor Robbie – he sank to his knees and began to cry like a baby.

I burst into tears. Mother rushed across to embrace her poor boy. Mrs Everington gave Robbie a look which I can only describe as utter hatred, mingled no doubt with relief that it wasn't her boy blubbing on the sitting room floor. 'I said it was a bad idea, sending a boy out there!' she screeched.

Father ordered everyone out. I didn't need telling. I fled upstairs to my room and wept and wept. I had ruined everything. I had turned the family pride into shame!

One thing was dreadfully clear to me – our Robbie was a broken man. What terrible things had happened to him over there? He was always so strong and brave! Surely, I thought, it must be this dreadful War and the horrible machines they use to fight it that has done him in. And if it's happened to Robbie, it could happen – must happen, has happened – to all the other young men too. Because the thought – the thought that Robbie alone . . .

I won't say it. It can't be true.

* * *

That night, when all was still, I crept into his room to beg forgiveness. He looked so white and useless lying there, I couldn't help but think that if it was men like this we depended on, we were going to be hard pressed to win. But I pushed such thoughts out of my mind. I had come to comfort him and not to judge, even though – I must be honest – my belief in him was shaken.

'Oh, it's you, Effie,' he said; and he blushed – with shame, I'm sure.

'I'm so sorry – I really put my foot in it, didn't I?' I said.

'The fault was mine. I just wasn't expecting... After all that noise at the Front, I was expecting quiet here at home,' he said; but I couldn't meet his eye.

'Weren't you in hospital for a good while?' I asked.

'Yes, but they started shelling positions just front of us and, you know, Effie, how I always hated loud bangs, ever since I was little. Just before I was wounded we had three weeks of it, three weeks of constant shelling – the bloody things whizzing overhead and blowing up all around us and... and...'

And, bless me, poor Robbie, he started weeping again.

I stayed with him an hour that night and he told me some terrible things, about how men die, and the stink, and the pain, and so on. But I could not answer – I could not! All it did was confirm my very worst fears. These things are to be expected in war. They didn't shock me. No, it was Robbie who shocked me. Robbie – my brave, gallant Robbie – was a coward! I would never stop loving him, of course, but I cannot tell you how ashamed I was – for myself, for our family, for our country, but most of all, for him.

'Don't think badly of me, Effie,' he begged. 'Other fellows get their nerves shot to pieces as well. We all need to escape after a time.'

On and on he rattled, but he must have known what I felt. The truth is, if I was him, I would rather be dead, killed a hundred times over, than to come home turned into this yellow creature, this white-feather crybaby.

But – but! If I am to work in the ambulances I shall have to put up with such stuff. There can be no judgement in the medical services, no putting one before the other. All are sick – the brave, the cowardly, the enemy even. So I held his hand and listened while he excused himself. I swore I understood, and that he would get better like any other soldier and soon be back in the thick of it, earning medals for his country and his family.

I tried to tell him my own plans – how I was going to make it to the Front to nurse the men and drive an ambulance. Of course, he did everything he could to dissuade me. The Front was no place for a girl, he said – for him of all people to make that claim! – and it was full of bad language – which made me laugh as well, for he had brought that very language into our sitting room! – and he was fearful I would be dishonoured. 'The girls who go out there often sink very low,' he said. 'It is odd how morals tend to fall away when there is so much death and destruction about.'

I put my chin up and told him there was no fear of that,

not while I was alive, unless my honour was taken against my will – and that is a risk every woman must take if she is to fare bravely in this world. He tried to make me promise not to go, but my mind was made up more firmly than ever. There was no getting away from it – Robbie had let us down. It was up to me to make up for his failings.

I had a plan afoot. I had read in the papers about Mrs Huntley, the suffragette, who had put aside her militancy for the War effort and was taking a band of like-minded women over to the Front to nurse the wounded right on the edges of the battlefields. That was the stuff for me! It was all to be done unofficially, of course, because the authorities were all frowning away desperately on women at the Front, especially suffragettes. But as Mrs Huntley said in the newspapers, if you left it up to the men, they would let the world fall to bits rather than allow a woman to help them. So women were making their own way – taking their own provisions and using their own money – even though the generals and politicians and clergy shrieked hysterically at them to stop.

Mrs Huntley was leaving from Dover on the Thursday evening. That gave me a few days at home to practise my nursing skills on poor Robbie and say goodbye to my family – in my own way, of course; they would only know what I had been doing after I had gone. If they had even the slightest inkling of my plans, they would certainly have locked me in a tower like Rapunzel!

* * *

Of course, Mrs Everington was around the very next day after Robbie had disgraced himself, full of understanding. She had an article with her about shell shock, and how even the bravest and most willing soldiers can fall foul to it.

'It is one of the sufferings of modern warfare, like a wound, if not quite so noble,' she explained. It could happen to anyone and she only thanked God that her son Howard hadn't suffered in the same way. She put it down to her grandfather having been such a notable soldier.

Then we all had to listen to her for half an hour, lecturing us in great detail about how aristocratic blood, like her grandfather's for example, had been bred for centuries to cope with the shocks of warfare but that other blood lines couldn't be expected to cope so well. Which inspired me to point out that half the country must have aristocratic blood in their veins, too, because it was well known that aristocrats – like her grandfather, for example – did tend to stray from the marital fold somewhat, didn't they?

My mother sent me out rather hurriedly on an errand, but not before giving me one of her most arch looks and a little nod of approval. Normally, marital relations are something we never discuss in this house – but when it comes to taking Mrs Everington down a peg or two, exceptions can be made.

When I came back in they were discussing a new military weapon: liquid fire, a kind of blazing fluid that burns the enemy to ashes on the spot. It sounded just the thing! The three of us raised our teacups and prayed to God that we might get lots and lots of it, to send those German soldiers back down to where they came from, and where the Devil himself no doubt keeps a good supply of it to keep them entertained for the next few thousand years.

On the day, I was up at dawn. I'd told Mother and Father I was off to visit my cousin Lizzie. They'd given me money for my fare, which made me feel bad, but it was the only way. I only hope they'll understand once they have time to think about it. Every nurse and, especially, every female driver who gets to the Front releases a man to fight. One of our brave Englishmen are worth five Bosch, I heard Father say the other day, so by doing this I am adding five soldiers on our side. Unless of course those soldiers are like poor Robbie, whose nerves are so shot, I wonder if he will ever recover. Every night, I hear him raving in his sleep. It makes me wonder how brave I will be, with the same blood flowing in my veins. But even as a child I was more daring and bold than Robbie. Whenever I have doubts I tell myself to keep faith – in my country, in my family, in myself, and in womankind. I shall prevail!

I caught up with Mrs Huntley at the docks, ready to depart. She was a little doubtful at first, because of my age – even though I'd added a year to make the magic eighteen. But her doubts melted away when I showed her the letter from my mother, blessing me and my enterprise, praising my abilities as a driver, a nurse and a hard worker with a stout heart –

and hoping that Mrs Huntley would take me on board!

'And if the boys can fight at eighteen, why cannot I nurse them, Mrs Huntley?' I demanded.

I knew that appealing to her suffragette instincts would pave my way. She held out her hand. 'Welcome aboard, my dear – we have need of more like you,' she said. I jumped up the gangplank and that was it. I was part of the team.

Many months later I told her how I'd forged that letter from my mother, and she forgave me at once. By then, I'd already made myself indispensable.

It took us a little over two months to set up our base, in the face of much lip-curling from both French and English generals, who clearly thought us weak and silly women, unable to cope with the stress of the Front.

'Go home, my dear, and sit still. We'll have no women at the Front,' one said to Mrs Huntley.

She looked him in the eye and hit straight back. 'You will have heard of childbirth before now,' she replied. 'But of course having a life burst out from inside of oneself is something a man would suffer gladly every day if it stopped him having any kind of serious competition from women. Your poor manhood would wither at the very thought.'

How I adore her! They just stood there like idiots and gaped at her. So we got little help but managed anyway, as women will.

The plan was to set up a Forward Dressing Station, where the wounded would be brought straight from off the battlefield to be tended before being sent on to hospitals further away. We found a little house, literally yards away from the trenches. It had no roof, no windows – the shells had long ago seen to all that. Even the walls were full of cracks. It had been looted bare, but it was enough for us. We set up tarps to keep wind out and the rain off, and cleaned everything to within an inch of its life. We begged, borrowed, bought and stole mattresses, sheets, blankets, bandages – and set about our work.

* * *

I look back now and wonder that this was just six months ago – six months! What a child I was! Sometimes I wonder if I'm even human any more. I can't dismiss my enthusiasm and desire to help, but how I wish I had been born at a time when such things might have been of use, and not in an age when every human virtue is being blown to pieces on the battlefield.

I've learned a great many things on the Front. How not to faint at the sight of blood. How not to retch at the stink of a man's insides. How to smile and look hopeful when a boy no older than I am asks me if he's going to be all right, when there are already flies crawling on his liver.

Oh, yes – and I have learned not to cry. Not a single tear has fled my eye since the first week, when I truly believed I would drown in them. I realised that if I started again, I would never stop. It worries Mrs Huntley though. She is desperate for me to shed a tear. I told her about Robbie and how I was resolved not to cry, because tears were for babies.

She scolded me and said that the tears of the brave were worth more than diamonds. I didn't believe it at the time. I do now.

How I will be able to face Robbie when I see him again? The way I spoke to him – the thoughts I had! How could I? I know better now, but no amount of knowing better will ever erase the memory of how I was unable to meet his eye. I thought bravery consisted of knowing no fear, but I understand now that it is not fear but utter terror that is the lot of every soldier, and that enough shelling will turn any man into a jelly.

And Mother! And Father! And Mrs Everington! What on earth will I say to them when I go home, if I survive? No one can ever understand who has not been here. I would like to curse them to their faces for sending their sons away to Hell, but no one will ever hold them to account, because they know no better, and the words do not exist that can describe this place. Only the knowledge that I was as bad as them will stop me spitting in their faces.

Oh, Mother and Mrs Everington – how shameless you would think me now! Did you know that I can clean up a man from head to foot without so much as blushing? Imagine what a hussy I've become. And the language! The words Robbie used in the sitting room that day seem so mild now. I'm only astonished that he managed to contain himself so well.

I wish I could show you around, Mother and Mrs Everington, to see our work here, tending these young men torn to pieces mentally and physically while the old men at home go to work to earn the money to keep them here, and the woman knit or learn to drive in order that one more boy can be freed up to have his insides blown out of him. You see that chap over there, gasping and coughing, Mother and Mrs Everington? What a mess he makes – scarcely the kind of thing we'd want in the drawing room, I think. Don't worry – we'll keep him here until he stops, so you won't have to see it. There he goes again. You'd think he might put a hand to his mouth, if he had any manners at all. And look at the nasty mess he spits out – green and pink. Disgusting. Have you ever seen the like? What on earth can it be, do you suppose? Some new type of cough breeding here in the trenches, do you suppose?

It's his lungs, Mother. Gas does that – it melts the lungs and while the remaining part of them produces mucus, the rest gets coughed up with the sputum, one piece after another; green and pink. Of course, the Germans get gassed too – marvellous isn't it, ladies, that we are doing such dreadful things to another mother's son in the name of our country? Does it make you proud, Mother? How about you, Mrs Everington? How you must have wept when you heard that your poor Howard had died. Gas, was it? You're not sure? Don't worry – you won't be told. It's a question of morale, you see. The boys at the Front won't want you to be worrying about them – it might slow down the production of scarves, mightn't it? And that would never, ever do!

Oh, and look at this boy who has come in! He has no face, Mother. How could he have been so careless as to lose it, I wonder. Oh, yes, of course – liquid fire, that's what did it. What a shame – the Germans have it as well. See that featureless stump wagging to and fro on his neck, wondering why he can't see or hear or talk. What is it the Bard says? 'Sans teeth, sans eyes, sans taste.' 'Sans life' very soon too. And I think he will be glad of it. I wonder if I should help him on his way? Oh, yes, I've done that, too. There are times when even the most urgent of God's commandments melt before the cruelty of man, and we have to learn a new moral code especially for this place.

I am not sure if the boy is English, French or German. His uniform has been burned off him. Odd how they all look the same when their uniforms and faces are burned away. Either way, we shall treat him just the same. Do you want to know why, Mother? Mrs Everington? It's because I no longer particularly care who wins this bloody war. I no longer care, because whoever is proclaimed the victor, I am sure of only one thing – we will all have lost.

There was the most fearful battle nearby yesterday. I was one of the first to get out there – I usually am, because I'm the best driver we have. We found the wounded in a turnip field and gathered them up, like turnips themselves, I thought. We sent ambulance after ambulance back, all four of them, loaded to the gills, and then back again, all four.

And again. It was right at the end that I found the boy, hidden quietly behind a heap of earth. He'd heard us but kept quiet, scared of what we might do to him. German, you see. Scared as a mouse of what we might do to him – as if it hadn't been done already!

The ambulances were all away so I sat and waited with him for them to come back. I gave him some water and we talked a very little in my poor German and his only slightly better English. But we made sense. Can you imagine – he'd joined up early too, poor boy. It seems the Germans are infected by the same disease we are.

We smoked a cigarette and talked about our countries, and we agreed that it was still possible to love one's country without agreeing with it in any shape or form and whilst sincerely despising the donkeys who rule it.

He was quiet for a bit and I started to think about what was waiting for me when I got back to the station. I think that was my mistake. Anyway, this boy, this German, he started to cry. It was the most horrible noise, a dreadful, high-pitched whining. It really got on my nerves for some reason – God knows why, it isn't as though I hadn't heard men weeping and screaming in pain before.

'Now, come on, that won't do,' I told him – which was unfair of me, because how could he help it? I tried to comfort him, but nothing seemed to help. He just lay there, staring off, making this terrible noise.

Then the shells started up again, sweeping across our turnip field, bombing the dead, blowing up the living – who knows why they do it? Just to terrorise each other, I suppose. Down they came, all around us, like some kind of devilish rain. It hurts your nerves, it really does. You can't hear a thing and you never know if one is going to land right by you, you see.

Anyway, the noise of the shells was really getting to this lad, because he screamed louder than ever. It was quite unbearable. I thought, Well I can't just sit here waiting while the poor beggar goes mad, can I? There's only one thing to do. I have to get out of it.

After a lot of huffing and puffing I managed to heave him over my shoulders – he wasn't so big fortunately – and off we went, staggering over the turnip field with the shells going off all around us. I know it sounds crazy, but I thought, Well, if one of them's got my number on, it's going to get me anyway. I didn't see the point of sitting waiting for it. It can bloody well come and find me, I thought!

I staggered along God knows how far before it did – finally. I don't know how far away it landed, but there was a noise like all hell blowing up. It blew both of us up in the air and we came down in a great storm of mud and clay. A great clod of it landed on my face and half stunned me, but other than that, I seemed to be all right.

'Well, if that's all that being hit with a shell does, I don't mind it so much,' I said to myself. I just lay there for a while. I thought the German boy must have died, but then, God help me, he started up again, that dreadful noise worse than ever. You never heard anything like it, I couldn't bear to listen to it. I couldn't work out where he was at first, until I realised it was coming from beneath me. I'd come down right on top of him.

The shelling had stopped by this time, but nothing I could say or do made any difference, he just kept on and on and on until I wanted to just bloody strangle him. I dug him out of the earth – it was a real effort, he was no help at all – and set off again over the turnip field with the screaming boy on my back.

I hadn't gone far when I heard a shout. It was Gillian and Sylvia come back from the station with the ambulance at last. 'You took your time,' I said.

They put me on a stretcher, carted me off to the ambulance and shoved me in. Off we went, with Sylvia sitting next to me, stroking my hair. It annoyed me, to be honest, because all this time the German lad was still making that God-awful noise, and all she could do was sit next to me, when I was pretty well all right except for a swollen face, which, believe me, is nothing.

'Can't you give him something for the pain, Sylve?' I asked her. 'That noise is driving me mad. I've been listening to it for hours now.'

'What noise? Who?' she asked.

'That poor boy, can't you hear him? He must be in the most terrible pain to be making a noise like that.'

'That boy you were with, Effie?' she said. 'That boy was dead. He'd been dead for a couple of days by the look of him. He isn't even in the ambulance with us.'

Well, that was ridiculous. I could hear him as clear as a bell.

'Sylve, what's wrong with you? Can't you hear it, that ruddy awful noise he's making?' I asked her.

She gave me a funny look and said, 'Effie, that's you, darling. That's you crying.'

'It can't be me!' I said, but she insisted it was.

Of course I refused to believe it. We argued about it all the way back to the station where they fetched Mrs Huntley to see if she could convince me. She came at once and gave me a sad old smile. 'Here they are, here they are, your precious tears at last,' she said, wiping my face.

I knew then that it was true.

She gave me a hug and told me that no girl had given as much as I had, and that she was sorry she'd waited so long, but now I was going home for a while. Then she tucked me up in bed and went to make arrangements for me to leave the next day.

Sky Dancer

by Berlie Doherty

Sky Dancer

'Are you going to sing with us, Kate?'

The small group of amateur performers was rehearsing a Christmas concert for their family and friends. Fred had organised it. He was a law student, but really he wanted to be a dancer. He could dance so his feet sounded like the pattering of rain, and then the beating of drums, and then the roll of thunder; and suddenly he would stop, poised like a bird in mid-flight, and sing without a hint of breathlessness.

Kate was very nervous about singing, especially in front of Fred. The only way she could do it was to pretend that he wasn't there. So she closed her eyes, her hands clenched tightly at her sides, and tremulously began, struggling to steady the shiver in her voice. She sang her mother's favourite song, 'A Bird in a Gilded Cage'. The other performers stopped chattering and looked at each other, surprised by the natural strength and sweetness of her voice. They gave her a spontaneous cheer of support and smiled across at her as she sat down again, trembling now with nerves. Sadie patted her hand and joined two other girls to practise their 'Three Little Maids from School' routine.

Fred came over and sat next to her. 'You have a lovely voice,' he whispered.

'Thank you,' she said, blushing.

'But no one will hear you in the hall if you sing as quietly as that.'

'Oh.'

He brushed the dark flop of his hair away from his eyes. 'You have to learn to project your voice. I bet you can, really. I think there's a lot of power in your voice if you weren't so nervous.'

Kate bit her lip. She could sing much more powerfully than that, she knew. Sometimes, when she was quite sure she was on her own she would let her voice really float out, just for the joy of hearing its sound. But it would seem like showing off to do it in public. It was as if she had two voices really; the quiet one and what her father called the 'belter'.

'I've got an idea,' he said. 'How would you like to do a duet with me?'

'With you? But I'm not good enough. You've just said, my voice isn't strong enough.'

'Don't be timid,' he said earnestly. 'I know it took a lot of courage to stand up and sing in front of all of us just now. But you proved you can do it, and I think you should let more people hear you.' He looked away and then back again, grinning. 'I think if you sing with me you won't feel so lonely on the stage. Shall we try?'

He sent the Three Little Maids off to get a cup of tea and sat down at the piano. He played the opening chords of 'Silent Night' and Kate began to sing, very softly, because it was even harder to perform just for Fred.

'Louder,' he said. 'My grandmother's coming tonight and she's deaf. Sing so the hairs on the back of her neck tremble like reeds in the wind.'

Kate giggled, but managed to keep on singing, and then Fred slipped his voice into hers, supporting her first with the same melody, and then, as she began to sound more confident, sliding into harmony. She let her voice ring out, pure and strong, thrilling at the sound of the music they were creating together.

'Good grief! You really *can* sing!' he said when they had finished. 'What a voice! We'll do that tonight and we'll bring the house down.'

She couldn't eat that evening; when she walked back to the hall with Sadie she was silent and tense with nerves and doubt. The only thing she knew for sure was that she didn't want to make a fool of herself in front of Fred. She was excited, too, because she would be standing next to him on the stage – she alone of all the people in the company would be singing with him.

She hardly heard any of the other performers as the concert progressed. At last Fred caught her eye and held out his hand to her. She joined him on the stage, her breath quaking like a trapped bird in her throat. 'Breathe steadily.

Take your time,' he murmured, and she nodded to him and smiled. She was ready. Their voices wound round each other, and then he stopped singing and gave her a solo. Her voice had never sounded so full and rich before. She let it soar. Her eyes were open and sparkling; for the first time in her life she knew the absolute joy of singing to a silent, rapt audience; she knew the sweetness of applause. Fred squeezed both her hands in his own and kissed them.

As they walked home together after the concert he edged his hand into hers again. She pretended not to notice.

'I wish the show would go on,' she said. 'I'd like to sing it lots more times with you.'

'Ah, Kate. Sweet Kate. You must carry on singing,' he said. They stopped under the cascade of light from a gas lamp. 'But not with me. Sing and sing, and think of me every time.'

'Why not with you?' she asked, deeply disappointed.

'Because I've signed up.' He lifted her hands to his lips. 'I'm going to the War.'

'You've signed up! But I don't want you to go,' she blurted out. 'I don't want you to be a soldier.' She turned away, clenching her hands, clenching her eyelids against the rush of hot tears, clenching her throat against the tremble of her voice.

He put his hands on her shoulders and turned her round to look at him. 'I'm not going to be a soldier. I've joined the Royal Flying Corps. I'm going to be an airman.'

'Not an airman, Fred! That's so dangerous!'

'I know how to fly. A couple of years ago my uncle and I

built a triplane – well, it looked more like a bicycle with wings – but I learned to fly it and I love it! I'm crazy about flying! Now our country needs airmen and I've signed up. I can't wait to be there. Part of it all. When you watch birds flying, think of me. Sky dancing!'

She smiled, caught up in his excitement, then shook her head. 'But you'll be so exposed up there. I can't bear to think of it.'

'All the same, what the airmen do is very important. They spy from above. They see the enemy lines. They bring back essential information.'

'Will you write to me?' she asked, awkward. After all, they hardly knew each other.

'Oh yes!' His face was close to hers now. She could feel the warm flutter of his breath on her cheek. 'I'd love that. And when I come home, we'll sing together.'

Fred wrote to her every other day, letters full of nonsense and fun about his training. She shared his letters with Sadie, giggling over his jokes and his funny spidery drawings. He's having a good time, she thought. I shouldn't have worried about him.

And then, two weeks later came the letter that she had been dreading. He really was going to war.

Dear Kate,
It's been fun with the chaps here. I've learned a bit more about flying. My uncle's triplane is like a butterfly

149

compared with the great dragonfly I'm piloting here. But, by Jove, she doesn't half rattle! Had my first solo flight today. I'm free! Free! I'll dance for you over the fields of France. Tomorrow, Kate! I sail to France tomorrow!

Your sky dancer,
Fred

She kept that letter under her pillow, taking it out to read whenever Sadie wasn't in the room. He sounded so happy, so full of life. 'Your sky dancer' he had signed it. She stroked the words. Was he really hers? Was that how he felt about her? And yet they had hardly spoken. They had sung together once. Held hands once. And when he had left her at her door that night of the concert, there had been a swift, shy kiss. He's safe with the Royal Flying Corps, she told herself. She'd heard about soldiers in the trenches, crawling through mud, itchy with lice. She'd heard about grenades being thrown at them, blowing them to pieces as if they were made of seashells, nothing more. Fred was safe from all that. Safe. He would be safe.

Fred's letters from France came frequently at first, some-times daily. He still spattered them with comical drawings of himself in his plane, flying upside down or dancing on the wings, blowing kisses at her. But as the war progressed, the tone seemed to change. The letters gave little news of what he was doing, though she knew that censors would block any real information. She searched them for hints of how he felt, away from her, but there was little of that either. There was a grim sort of cheeriness to his writing, a detachment from the War itself. It was as if he didn't see himself in any danger, or didn't care about it if he was. She tried to imagine the happy, dancing young man she had fallen in love with, but he wasn't there in his letters now. And his image was slipping away from her – she couldn't even remember what he looked like any more. The letters began to be less frequent. He's too busy to write, she told herself. Or maybe he doesn't think about me now. When his letters did come, she ran upstairs to read them in private. There was nothing that she wanted to share with Sadie now.

'Lost my gunner today,' he wrote tersely one day. 'Pity. Nice chap.'

She read his letter again, bewildered by his tone. 'Pity'? A life lost, and it was a *pity*? Was that all he could say about a man who had died? Was Fred really so callous? Is that what war had done to him?

And it was news to her that Fred flew with a gunner. She thought he did reconnaissance flights. Why hadn't he told her before? What did they shoot? Other aeroplanes? Was that what Fred did? What if he had been shot along with his gunner? She had a picture in her head of a plane spiralling out of the sky like sycamore wings. She was cold with the terror of it. Maybe it happened all the time that aeroplanes were shot down, that fellow airmen died. But how could he be so callous as to write in such a way? She tried to reply, and couldn't think of any response to make. He must have had to carry on flying with his gunner dead in the plane with him. Maybe he was still being shot at while there was no one to defend him. What would have happened when he landed the plane? Did he just walk away from it and find another man to replace the gunner? 'Pity. Nice chap'? Didn't he care at all?

She kept starting a letter and not finishing it. She was haunted by the idea of him flying in a plane with a dead man beside him, and not caring. I don't know him, she told herself. I thought I loved him, but I don't really know him at all. She had no idea what to write about now. He has nothing to say to me, she thought, and I have nothing to say to him; here, safe in Liverpool, working in a shop. What has Fred's war to do with me? I was just hanging on to a dream, but I don't really know what that dream was. That's it. He was just a dream.

I will write back, she thought, folding away his letter yet again. But not yet.

'Oh, but keep him safe!' she whispered. 'Fred. Be safe.'

Not long after this, one of the Three Little Maids from the Christmas concert came into the grocery shop where she worked. Kate was weighing out tea for her when the girl said, 'Did you hear about poor Fred Sweeney?'

Kate was suddenly chilled to the bone on that hot Monday morning. Tea leaves trembled from the scoop, pattering back into the tin like dry tears. Don't tell me, she thought. Don't say anything. Don't give me words.

'Shot down. They didn't even find his body. Poor Fred.'

Kate stared after the girl as she left the shop. Flies were buzzing against the window; shoppers strolled by. I've lost him. He's gone. I never wrote back to him. And now he's gone.

Feathers in the air. Dancing bird stilled in flight.

After that Kate went inside herself and nobody could reach her, not even Sadie. There were no giggled secrets at bedtime. No singing. She put Fred's letters away in a tin box and hid it under the bed. If only she had replied to his letter – just one last letter, maybe he would have received it before his plane was shot down. All she had needed to say to him was: Fred. Be safe. For me. Please be safe. But she hadn't written, and he never knew how much she cared. 'I loved you,' she whispered. 'And you never knew.'

'You can't go on like this,' Sadie told her. 'He's gone, Kate. You can't keep grieving for him. Nearly everybody we know has lost somebody now; the whole country would come to a stop if they all gave in like you. You didn't really know him, after all. You have to find something to do. Something to take your mind off him.'

'I'll never take my mind off him,' Kate muttered. 'I want to follow him. I want to go to France.'

'How?' Sadie laughed. 'As an airman? A soldier?'

'He gave up his life for people like us. I don't even know

what happened to him. How can I just sit here and do nothing?'

'You could do what Mum and I are doing, and work down in the munitions factory like all the women. Leave the shop.'

'Munitions? More weapons for killing people?'

Sadie stared at her, astonished. 'For killing the *enemy*, Kate.'

But she knew Sadie was right. She had to get out of the house. It stifled her. She couldn't go back to work in the shop, where she would forever hear the dry patter of tea leaves that had accompanied the news of Fred. Besides, her job had gone to a young mother who had just lost her husband. She wandered aimlessly round the streets, and paused to read a notice board outside the YMCA.

Miss Lena Ashwell is seeking artistes to form concert parties to entertain the forces in France. Professional performers only to apply. Auditions today between 9 a.m. and noon.

She read and reread it; excited and dazed. She knew the name; Lena Ashwell was a famous actress. She and Sadie had seen her at the Playhouse. What kind of 'artistes' was she looking for, Kate wondered. Singers? If only she could apply!

She forced herself away from the board, telling herself it was nothing to do with her, but she couldn't stop thinking about it. It would be a way to do it, a way to go to France. She would be doing something to help. Surely making music was better than making weapons? She might even find out what had happened to Fred. She would be walking on the same soil as him, under the skies of France. It would be a way of saying a final goodbye.

But she was far from being a professional. She hadn't had any training. She didn't even have any sheet music; everything she had learned was from the recordings that her father listened to on his great horned gramophone, mostly Gilbert and Sullivan, but some Italian and French operas too. She knew the arias off by heart.

But she was too shy, surely?

She sat on the wall opposite the YMCA hall, her legs dangling over a snoring dog. She watched people walking in and out carrying violins, briefcases of music, suitcases of costumes. Noon approached; it was her last chance. Panicking, she jumped off the wall and went inside. After all, nothing worse could happen than if they turned her down.

When she went in, the two women who were conducting the auditions looked bored and tired. One of them was sitting at a piano, shuffling together sheets of music. The other she recognised as the famous actress herself, and immediately felt too much in awe to speak. They must have chosen their performers already, she told herself, and were longing for twelve to strike so they could go home. *I won't bother them.* She turned away, crestfallen. How on earth would she have the courage to sing?

'Ah, just in time!' Miss Ashwell said brightly. 'I hope you're a singer?'

Kate turned in her tracks. She nodded and swallowed. No backing out now.

'Your name?'

'Kate Hendry.' It was scarcely more than a whisper.

'No music?' the woman at the piano said crossly.

'Just sing anything, dear,' Miss Ashwell said, more gently.

Kate tried to remember everything Fred had told her: breathe slowly, take your time, fill the hall. Remember my deaf grandmother. She began to sing, gently, as if he was standing behind the two women, listening. She sang him the Christmas song they had performed together, imagining his light voice weaving around hers.

'Pretty girl, pretty voice,' Miss Ashwell said.

The pianist picked out a sheet of music from her pile and began to play softly. Kate recognised the aria straight away: 'One Fine Day' from *Madame Butterfly*. She smiled at Miss Ashwell and started to sing. Now Fred was at the back of the hall; she would fill the space between them with her powerful voice. *For you, Fred. Hear my voice.*

'Oh, wonderful! You're just about perfect, dear!' Miss Ashwell stood up and grasped Kate's hands warmly. 'We were short of a soprano to make up a new concert party, and here you are!'

'Not married are you?' the pianist asked.

Kate shook her head, overwhelmed with the enormity of what was happening.

'That's good. Can't send ladies whose husbands are already over there.' She checked her list and looked up briskly. 'We'll write to you, Miss Hendry. You'll be travelling with a contralto, Miss Rowena Rumble, of whom you have no doubt heard? The fine tenor Mr Donald Bentley and the acclaimed bass baritone Mr Arthur Poacher make up the quartet. You will be singing duets and quartets from the operas with them, as well as solos, and you will be accompanied by a pianist. You will have one week's rehearsal with the other members of your party. They are all professional, very talented.'

'I know you lack experience, Miss Hendry,' Miss Ashwell interrupted. 'But what a voice! Such a surprise, my dear! Our men out there will be thrilled to hear it, and completely charmed by a young pretty girl like yourself. It's what they need. Good music to cheer their hearts, pretty smiles to remind them of their sisters and sweethearts. It won't be easy. Some of your concerts will be in base hospitals, you realise? Oh, and there'll be an entertainer – conjuror, juggler, comedian or something like that.' Her voice tailed away – Kate was already over there; she was already singing.

The Channel crossing was dreadful. Too sick to go downstairs, Kate stayed on deck wrapped in rugs, watching how the waves lurched up as the ship lurched down, praying she would not die before she reached French soil. The other members of the concert party had retired downstairs. The huge, disdainful contralto Miss Rowena Rumble had turned a pale shade of green as soon as she had stepped on board. 'Why do I do this?' she had moaned. 'There'll be nothing left of me by the time we reach France!' The shy, fussy pianist Peter Castleton was anxiously guarding his portable piano, which he called 'Little Peter'. Mr Poacher sat with his handkerchief over his face, groaning softly to himself, and remained like that for the whole crossing.

Halfway through the voyage Kate was joined by Donald Bentley, the tenor. She had been surprised to see how young he was; not much older than herself. She thought all the young men had been called to fight; only conscientious objectors stayed away, and they were pilloried for cowardice. He lurched across the deck, holding his bowler hat firmly on his head with both hands. When he reached Kate he removed it and held it across his chest like a shield. 'May I join you, Miss Hendry?'

He lowered himself down awkwardly next to her and sat with his leg stretched out in front of him. 'So happy, so happy to be going to France at last!' he said. 'Wanted to fight like any man. Army turned me down. Have this gammy leg, you see.'

Kate nodded, embarrassed. It was as if he had been reading her mind. He was obviously embarrassed too; keen to put her right. His speech was jerky and breathless, as if he was anxious and ill at ease.

'Can't run. Can't kneel. No good for a soldier – even though most of the poor blokes come home worse than me. Couldn't live with myself, stuck at home while pals were off to France. But God gave me a voice. I can use it to help somebody through a bad time. Like you. The boys will love you. Excuse me. Don't mean to embarrass you. Please call me Donald. There!' He patted her hand lightly, and she nodded her thanks.

I don't want anyone to love me, she thought. I just want to breathe the air that Fred breathed.

'What made you decide to come over, may I ask? You're so young. It's very brave of you.'

She looked away. No, she wasn't ready to tell anyone about Fred, not yet. The words wouldn't come. 'Like you,' she muttered. 'I just wanted to help.'

She stood up quickly, forcing back the familiar surge of tears, and went to look over the ship's railings. On the distant horizon, a dark lumpy shape was looming through the mist and spray.

'France,' said Donald, joining her. 'We're nearly there, at last!'

The company finally staggered out at Boulogne; Mr Poacher and Mr Castleton supported Miss Rumble, who was dabbing at her mouth with a handkerchief. Charlie the Chuckler tottered down the gangway like a drunken man, exaggerating his relief at being on dry land. Donald smiled at Kate. 'All right, Miss Hendry?'

'Fine, thank you.' She clenched her hands together. I'm here! she thought. Fred, if only you knew! I'm with you!

They were met by an army truck and driven to the stationary hospital at Harfleur. Kate sat next to Miss

Rumble, who overflowed her portion of the seat and spent the journey pitching her rolling body against Kate's. It rained torrentially all the way there, and when they arrived the whole camp was like an estuary at low tide, sticky with thick mud. Mr Poacher supported a gasping Miss Rumble as they clambered over the slippery duckboards that led to the concert shed. Kate felt Donald's hand touching her arm, just briefly, just enough to steady her. Mr Castleton and Charlie the Chuckler and one of the officers struggled to carry Little Peter, which tinkled protest at every step. Exhausted, they sank it onto the rickety tables that had been lashed together to form a stage.

'We'll never fill this place,' Kate said, gazing round the lofty shed.

'Oh, you will,' the officer assured her. 'The men have been talking of nothing else for days. I'll send soup and sandwiches for you, and I'll leave you to tune up and whatever it is you do before a concert. I tell you, we're so grateful to you for coming. All of you.' Kate noticed how he glanced at Donald, his face clouding slightly, and how Donald looked away, uncomfortable. 'It'll make the world of a difference to our lives out here.'

Kate was prickly with nerves. Charlie the Chuckler prattled through his jokes at top speed, pacing up and down the stage, gesticulating wildly, throwing in the occasional imitation of cows mooing and dogs barking. Miss Rumble appeared to be sleeping, breathing deeply and slowly, but every now and again her hands opened out expressively, like flowers, as though she was silently performing her repertoire. Arthur Poacher, the bass, played a solo card game. Donald hummed his way through his tunes. He smiled every time he caught Kate's glance. 'Don't be nervous,' he said. 'Once we get this first full concert over, we'll be fine.'

The officer who was looking after them put his head round the door. 'Thirty minutes to go,' he told them. 'Some of the men are on their way already.'

Miss Rumble opened her eyes. She caught hold of Kate's arm and pulled her towards the screen that had been set up for them. 'Get your stage frock on, young lady,' she ordered. 'Never let an audience see you in your day clothes. It spoils the illusion.'

Almost immediately, the soldiers began to flock into the shed in loud, excited groups. Kate peeped through a gap in the screen. The officers filled up the first rows of seats. Behind them came the men, a never-ending stream of them, some bandaged, some walking with sticks, some being helped along. Soon all the seats and benches were filled. They squatted in the gangways, stood in crammed, jostling packs at the back; able-bodied men clambered onto the shoulders of others and swarmed up onto the rafters, swinging along the beams and dangling their legs over like huge spiders. The doors at the back of the shed were pinned back wide to allow for hospital beds to be pushed into the gap. There was no longer a gap, and still men kept coming. The rain drummed onto the roof and spat between the

BERLIE DOHERTY

cracks, and the air was hot and buzzing with expectation and excitement.

Candles had been lit along the front of the stage, and one by one the lanterns that hung from the rafters were extinguished. The audience fell completely silent. Miss Rumble slid her sweating hand onto Kate's arm. 'If you're wondering why we do this,' she whispered, 'you're about to find out, Miss Hendry.'

The piano played the opening chords of 'God Save the King', and every man in the audience who could do so scrambled to his feet, took off his hat, and sang the national anthem. Kate had never heard such a swell of sound. Her throat clenched with unwonted emotion. Rowena Rumble let go of her arm and walked onto the stage. She sang 'Annie Laurie', and there wasn't a breath of sound from the audience. Rowena was overweight, greasy with sweat, well into her fifties, and full of self-importance – and she was magnificent. The applause at the end was like thunder.

It was the same for Mr Poacher, and for the duets he sang with Miss Rumble. In rehearsal they had never performed so well. Charlie the Chuckler trotted onto the stage, tripping over his trouser legs, which were far too long. His jokes had everyone groaning; the audience loved him. How wonderful it is, Kate thought, listening to the surge of laughter. They've all been through so much darkness, and yet they can still laugh at Charlie.

Now, it was Donald's turn. Like Kate, he had never been in one of these concert parties before. She was aware of the

162

bristle of his nerves as he stepped past her. 'Good luck,' she whispered involuntarily. There was a quiver and murmur among the audience when he first appeared, and then as he crossed to the centre of the stage to stand beside the piano she noticed that his limp had worsened, was exaggerated even.

Then she began to relax and so did the men in the audience. Donald's voice was very fine – much better than Fred's, she thought sadly. Fred. Fred. Why didn't I write to him again? Why didn't I ever tell him how I felt about him?

On Donald's third song some of the audience began to hum quietly along with him, and when he lifted his hand to encourage them, they joined in the chorus. At the end of his first set they cheered and stamped, won over with the power of music.

At last, it was Kate's turn. She pressed her hands to her face. 'This is for you, sky dancer,' she whispered. She took a deep breath, and as she stepped on stage there were low whistles of approval. Night had fallen fully. All she could see of the audience was the loom of white faces, like moons, along with a blue haze of tobacco smoke, and the glowing eyes of cigarettes and pipes. And right at the back of the shed, surely, surely, the ghost of Fred, smiling, encouraging; and she sang to him. She sang a song that every person in the hall would know, 'Ave Maria'. Her voice was full and rich; she no longer held it back. She had a natural power that amazed everyone in the room. She amazed herself.

The sound of the roars and cheers was never to leave her, nor the cheering at the end of the show, nor the babble of voices as the men left the shed and made their way, humming and whistling the tunes they had heard, back to their sleeping quarters and their lonely dreams.

'I can't thank you enough,' the officer told them as he helped them to load their luggage onto the army vehicle the next morning. 'Some of us have been to hell in the last few weeks. Some are waiting to go back there, and are bored with waiting, and frightened. Some of us will never see home again, and we know it – but you brought a piece of home to us last night. For three whole hours we forgot our misery.' He saluted them. 'Come back soon!'

There was a roaring sound in the sky; the throaty rumble of an aeroplane. Kate stood with her hands shielding her eyes, peering up into the sun that was blinding her. A triplane hovered like a moth before it disappeared into a cloud.

'Come on, come on!' Miss Rumble called to her. 'What's the matter with you, Miss Hendry? Time to move on.'

Kate was deeply moved by what the officer had said. They all were. As soon as they left the Harfleur Valley, the enormity of what they were undertaking seemed to overwhelm them. It was easy to forget the War when they were in England; to talk about it as though somehow, really, it had nothing to do with them. Now it had everything to do with them – it was part of their lives. They drove in silence through villages where every house was riddled with bullet holes; buildings destroyed, fields laid waste with muddy trenches. They saw horses covered with white blankets, silent and still, waiting to be taken to the fighting lines. They passed a long line of men, walking, muddy and ragged, some of them limping. They were coming back from the Front. How old they look, Kate thought. Old men. They look like a bunch of scarecrows. That's what the War has done to them.

Wherever they went, they had the same rapturous reception, whether they were in base camps or in hospitals. Sometimes their concerts would be in the open air because there was no room big enough to house all the men who were well enough to come. The flaps of the hospital tents would be pinned back so the patients in beds wouldn't miss anything. In other places they did two or three performances a day inside cramped huts. Kate finished each one dripping with perspiration, and by the end of the day she was completely exhausted. Her throat was tight and clenched with overuse and the stench of cigarette smoke.

Rowena suggested one evening that maybe they could take the music to some of the men who were too ill to be brought to the concert.

'Is anyone else willing?' she asked. 'Mr Poacher?'

The bass singer, Arthur Poacher, puffed out his cheeks. 'Matter of course, my dear Miss Rumble. I'm sure we all feel the same. And Mr Bentley? What about you, Mr Bentley? I'm sure you could *limp* along to the wards?'

There was a *frisson* among the party; everyone stared at

Donald. Kate tried to catch his eye, willing him to confirm to his colleagues that he was unfit to fight. She hated the way people looked at him wherever he went, as if they thought that he was malingering. What if he is though? she wondered to herself. What if he hates the thought of fighting so much that he's just pretending to be disabled? She felt a stab of sympathy, then chased the thought away. You can't just stand by and let other people do the fighting, she told herself. Fred didn't.

'Mr Poacher,' said Donald, 'I know what you are thinking. I know what everyone is thinking. All the young, fit men out there watch me walk on and think, Why isn't he with us, fighting? He's just a conchie. He's a coward. He should be covered with tar and feathers. I've heard it all before, Mr Poacher.'

'Now hold on,' Mr Castleton said, embarrassed. 'It's the Hun we want to fight, not each other.'

Rowena Rumble cleared her throat, interrupting the unpleasant banter. 'As I was saying, we could sing to the very sick men. The dying. How about you, Miss Hendry? Though I warn you, it may not be easy.'

Kate shook her head. All she wanted to do by then was to sleep. Besides, she hated the thought of walking amongst wounded and dying men. She would grieve for them; she would grieve for Fred. It would be impossible to sing.

She went out of the concert shed and made her way to her sleeping quarter. The sky was blazing with stars; lamps and lanterns glowed outside the sheds and tents. She could hear the low murmur of voices, the soft sound of someone playing a harmonica and, in the distance, the rich, full sound of Miss Rumble's voice beginning to sing inside the main hospital shed. She paused, suddenly overwhelmed by the strange beauty of it all. And there it was again; barely perceptible, the throaty sound of an aeroplane crossing the sky over her head. But surely she was mistaken? Planes didn't fly at night; she knew that. The sound faded away, and now she was aware of a dark shape moving towards her from the shadows. She gasped, clutching her hand to her mouth, haunted by ghosts.

'Miss Hendry? Kate?'

'Oh. It's you, Donald. I thought you were going to the ward?'

'I'm afraid Arthur Poacher and I do not get on well.'

'I gathered that.'

'You don't agree with him, do you?'

Kate paused, a fraction too long. Doubt chased across her mind and away again. 'I'm tired,' she said. 'Goodnight, Donald.'

He put his hand on her arm. 'Has Miss Rumble told you about Miss Ashwell's letter?'

Kate shook her head. She knew that there had been a letter. She had seen Miss Rumble deep in conversation with Mr Castleton and Mr Poacher about it. 'Are we being called back home?' She felt disappointed. I'm not ready yet, she thought. Not ready for that other life, that calm, distant world.

'The opposite. I overheard her saying that Miss Ashwell wants us to go on from here to entertain the troops on the Front Line.'

Kate pressed her hands together with a thrill of excitement. 'Really? How soon?' She remembered how eagerly Fred had written about going to France after his training. Yes, yes, the Front Line. This was what she had come for.

'You don't have to do this, you know. In spite of what Miss Rumble says. Being near the Front Line will be a terrifying experience. Not a good place for a young lady to be. If you want to go home, you can.'

'I don't.' Surprised by his suggestion, she swung back at him. 'What gave you that idea? I want to go! All these soldiers – some of them are younger than I am. I don't know what they really go through – none of us does – but I know enough now to admire their courage.' She faltered. A burst of noise came from one of the barrack sheds; boys, they were, sporting and joking, laughing and scrapping like the boys at home. 'They can't go home, can they? However much they might want to.'

'They'd get shot if they did. Look, Miss Hendry, I can speak to Miss Rumble for you, if you change your mind.'

She pulled herself away from him. She wished he didn't treat her like this, as if he was forever looking after her, as if he wanted to be more than just a friend. She wasn't ready for getting to know anyone else yet, not even a kind man like Donald. 'Goodnight, Mr Bentley.'

* * *

As they neared the Front, every day, every performance, became more harrowing, more tiring – more rewarding. It felt to Kate as if this was the only life there was; making music on the fringe of a brutal war, living in the unlikely company of the concert party. At home she would have chosen none of them as friends, except perhaps Donald. Even though his protectiveness annoyed her, there was a fragility about him, a defensiveness, a frail kind of pretend bravado that drew her to him, made her feel that he was the one who needed protecting.

On the day of their journey to the Front they were all tense, all thinking privately about what might happen, thoughts too frightening to give words to. Charlie started rehearsing his act as he always did, muttering his jokes to himself at impossible speed just under his breath, punching his fists together to give energy to the words.

'Give it a rest,' Mr Poacher snapped. 'You'll never learn those jokes if you don't know them by now.' Abruptly he turned to Kate. 'Did you lose someone, Miss Hendry? Is that why you're here with us?'

'There's not one of us who hasn't,' Rowena told him sharply. 'Not one of us. It doesn't do to talk about it.'

'Your young man, was it?' Arthur Poacher persisted. 'Was he a soldier?'

'He was an airman,' Kate whispered. It was the first time she had spoken to anyone here about Fred.

'God help the airmen,' Mr Poacher sighed. 'There's courage for you. Or madness. Imagine – you're in one of them kites up in the sky. Open cockpit. Sitting target. You get shot, your plane is on fire. Whoosh, up it goes. You can jump if you want to, but there's no parachute, of course. Not allowed. You die with your plane. Go out like a blazing comet.'

Donald leaned forward and grasped him by the shoulders. 'Enough!' he hissed.

Arthur Poacher stared at him, amazed. 'What do you know about it? Charlie here lost his brother and Mr Castleton lost his son, but they'd be out there on the Front Line if they were young enough to fight. So would I – I'd be willing to give up my life, if it came to it, just as Miss Hendry's young man did.'

'I say, Mr Poacher, I say,' Mr Castleton put in mildly. 'Not nice talk this, eh?'

Kate stared uncomfortably out of a slit in the canvas of the truck. It was an ugly argument; she didn't want to have anything to do with it. She wished Donald would defend himself instead of letting Arthur Poacher bully him.

But Mr Poacher was like a dog who'd dug up a meaty bone; he wouldn't let go. He glanced round triumphantly. 'Why did you join this concert party, Mr Bentley?'

'That's enough!' Rowena said sharply.

'Has anyone ever seen how bad his leg is?' Mr Poacher said. 'Undresses in the dark, dresses in the dark. That's what I've noticed.'

Donald stood up. His face was ash pale. He had a line of sweat on his upper lip. 'Excuse me, Miss Hendry. Excuse me,

Miss Rumble,' he said. Very slowly, he began to roll up his trouser hem, right up to the thigh. His leg was made of wood. 'I am not proud of this,' he said simply. 'I would dearly like to be whole again.'

Kate was embarrassed and shocked. She was ashamed that she had ever doubted him. She remembered his flustered, halting words when they had spoken on deck all those weeks ago. She had let him down; allowed herself to mistrust him just because others had. He had been too proud to defend himself, but surely she could have stood up for him instead of pretending it had nothing to do with her. He's my friend, she admitted to herself. He looks after me. He's a good man. And I let him down.

They travelled on in silence, each of them too wrapped up in their thoughts to speak, no one looking at anyone else. Arthur pretended to sleep. After a while Charlie the Chuckler began to hum very softly to himself with more of a yawn than a singing voice. He lifted his hands as if they were an audience, encouraging them to join him in his singing. Donald nodded and began to sing along. Relieved, Kate hummed softly. Rowena Rumble's beautiful contralto voice fluttered a low harmony. That left Arthur Poacher, still pretending to sleep, his eyelids flickering nervously. Charlie leaned forward and put his ear to Arthur's mouth, and at last, still with his eyes closed, the deep, rumbling bass joined in.

When they arrived at their venue they climbed out of the vehicle like people in a dream. Each of them had gone through their own private hell. Mechanically they prepared themselves for the first concert at the Front. For six weeks solid they had given two or three concerts a day, travelling miles between venues, sleeping in draughty huts and leaking halls, hostels and farmhouses, ancient châteaux and sometimes in the open air under a canopy of trees. They had seen unimaginable misery and boredom and pain. They were utterly exhausted. And yet they each had the feeling that this was what they had really come to do, that this near encounter with death and the men who faced it daily was the most important thing they had ever done in their lives.

'Here we are again, our merry little band of trouba-dours!' Charlie the Chuckler said as they unloaded their clothes, the minimal props, and lastly Little Peter.

'Come on, little chap,' the pianist said. 'A few more tunes, a few more songs, and I'll take you home again, eh?' He rubbed the keys with his handkerchief. 'Eighteen, my son was,' he said, to no one in particular. 'Brilliant pianist.' And then he fell again into that deep and lonely silence that had always kept him apart from the others.

Not far away, they could hear the *crump, crump* of firing. It was alarmingly close and persistent, impossible to ignore. Kate felt a slow, cold dread rising in her. So this was it. This was the sound of war.

The concert hall had been prepared for them, and they waited, restless, keen to get on with the job. Within hours of arriving they were ready to perform. Peter Castleton played endlessly while the hall was filling up; it was as if he needed to lose himself and his thoughts in his music. The men filed in, while their fellows and the enemy fought for their lives within earshot. Kate stood next to Donald, waiting for her turn. She could see the sweat on his upper lip, the tremble of his hands.

Charlie was on stage cracking his litany of jokes and impressions when the first shell landed so near that the hall shook. Nobody in the audience moved, but the members of the concert party froze in a silent terror. Charlie wiped his brow and carried on. Another shell. The tension on stage was like a tight skin, binding them, choking them. But still nobody moved, nobody spoke. Another shell. 'Shut up!' Charlie shouted. 'You're spoiling my punch lines.'

There was a roar of laughter and applause. Peter sprang to the piano and began to play some ragtime. The four singers clambered onto the stage. They sang arias from *Tosca* and *The Barber of Seville* along with music hall songs. The audience joined in and for one glorious hour, while the sound of shelling was drowned out, it was as if nothing in the world mattered except the music.

'Give them a solo, Kate,' Rowena said, and they left her alone on the stage.

She was wearing a red dress, her favourite. She knew she looked her best. She was aware of the intake of breath as she stepped forward. I am their sister, their daughter, their sweetheart, she told herself. They want me to smile at them, so they can smile at me. They want me to love them, so they can love me. They want me to be happy for them.

She could smell cigarette smoke and sweat and candle grease. Outside, muted now, she could hear the spattering of gunfire. Sing. Sing for Fred. The 'Gypsy Song' from *Carmen*. How he would love that!

When she had finished there was a long pause. Someone from the audience shouted, 'Marry me, miss!' and everyone cheered. She turned to look for Rowena to join her for the duet, and at that moment there was a thunderous shudder as though the whole building had collapsed around them. There were shouts of 'Evacuate!', the sound of chairs being pushed back, of people running, shouting.

Kate felt a hand grasp hers. 'Run!' Donald shouted, and suddenly, as if she had woken up out of a nightmare, she ran, Donald limping at her side, out of the concert hall, across a yard that was grey with smoke and dust, and into the metal shed that was used as their changing room. The rest of the company followed them, except for Peter. Donald turned to run back for him, but Arthur Poacher barred the way.

'Don't risk it. He'll be fine,' he said. 'Stay here, please, where it's safe.'

They all crouched down on their hands and knees, too frightened to speak. There were four gas masks in the corner. Four gas masks; six people. Donald grabbed one and held it out to Kate, but she shook her head. Rowena did the same. He dropped it back onto the floor. If they couldn't all wear one, no one would. This is how close we have become, Kate thought. We are a family now. She crouched, eyes closed, her heart pumping like a wild, hunted beast, and waited for the unimaginable end to come.

After all, there was no gas. The shelling stopped as suddenly as it had started. There was utter silence around them; the silence of exhaustion and relief; the silence of tense waiting.

At last Donald pushed open the door of their shed. He stood with his arms akimbo, gazing out at the fog of dust, and then they heard him say, 'The concert hall has been bombed. There's nothing left of it.'

'Oh, God. Peter!' Arthur said.

He ran towards the debris of the destroyed building, pushing past the soldiers who were trying to make it safe for rescuers. It was he and Donald who discovered Peter Castleton's body. He had died lying under the little piano.

'If you had gone for him, you would be dead too,' Arthur said. He held out his hand. Donald hesitated for a moment, then held out his own. The two enemies shook hands in grim, grieving silence.

'Bloody war. Bloody, bloody war. What the hell are we doing here anyway?' Charlie moaned when he joined them. 'I wish I was home.'

'It could have been any one us. All of us,' Kate said, her voice cold and tight with horror.

'We don't have to stay here, you know,' Donald whispered. 'I've told you, Kate. I'll help you to get home, if you would like. I want you to be safe.'

She shook her head, tears blinding her eyes. She thought of Peter running onto the stage to play the piano earlier that evening. She thought of the audience of soldiers singing with them, lustily, fearlessly, only hours ago. 'No, I want to stay,' she said.

It never got easier. Without a pianist they had to sing un-accompanied, though sometimes at the camps there were musicians who could work with them till Miss Ashwell found a replacement for Peter. As they were driven from base to base, Kate gazed blankly out of the truck, watching the lines of young, fresh, eager soldiers marching towards the Front; seeing draggled lines returning from it, grimy, wounded, dispirited, hobbling like old men. One of the wounded soldiers turned his head towards the truck as they rumbled past. His eyes rested for a moment on Kate. She tried to smile, lift a hand; and couldn't. She had seen too much of it, too many. The soldier looked away.

Yet, wherever they went, they set up their stage and lights and met with the same grateful reception from men in dread of what tomorrow would bring, men who had lost their friends, men who were close to death. Kate sobbed herself to sleep every night, and Rowena put her hand on her shoulder in silent support.

'If I had a daughter, I would want her to be like you,' Rowena said one day, after a concert. 'Courageous. It takes great courage to do things when you're afraid.'

'Aren't you afraid?' Kate asked.

'No. Just sad.'

'It's our turn to do the wards tonight, isn't it?'

'It is. These men here won't be going home, any of them. It will be very hard.'

'I know. I'll come.'

It was a pitiful task, to walk into the makeshift tent where the dying men lay, too ill to be moved on, fresh from the worst battle of their lives. The lamps were dim and flickering, giving the bandaged figures the appearance of ghosts. Some were lying completely still, eyes closed, waiting for the end to come. Others were groaning or shouting out in pain, but as soon as Rowena started to sing they fell silent, brought briefly back to a more beautiful place. There was no applause at the end, just a few gasped words of thanks.

Rowena touched Kate's hand. 'Now you, dear,' she said. 'Your voice might be the last thing they ever hear.'

Kate stepped into the middle of the tent and began to sing. There was no accompaniment, so she chose two simple songs from her repertoire. By the time she started the second, her courage had returned and she began to walk from bed to bed. It was the song she had used for the Christmas show at home – she hadn't sung it since. 'Silent Night' in the middle of summer. Holy night in the middle of hell. Peaceful night in the middle of war.

Now, in the listening silence, she could hear, very faintly, someone trying to hum a harmony. She moved towards the voice. A heavily bandaged man was lying on a bed, his face turned away from her. She broke off, suddenly and incredulously knowing the voice, rasping and painful as it was, knowing the harmony. He turned his head with great difficulty and opened his eyes.

'Fred?' she whispered.

Could this white, haggard face really be his? But he was dead. Surely.

Yet, hadn't she hoped, hadn't she known, that he was alive still? Wasn't that why, without admitting it to herself, she had come here, in the hope of seeing him again?

His hand struggled to touch hers.

'Ssh!' An orderly appeared beside her. 'Don't make him speak. Yes, his name is Fred. Do you know him?'

'Fred,' Kate murmured. She dared to touch his cheek. 'But his plane was shot down.'

'He landed in enemy territory. He's been in a prisoner of war camp and escaped – only to get caught up in this. We brought him in yesterday, very badly wounded. He's lost both his legs.'

Kate sank onto the floor beside the bed, her face so close to his that it was nearly touching. 'My sky dancer!' she whispered. Tears streamed down her cheeks.

'Surely this isn't your airman?' Rowena had come to stand behind her. 'Oh, my dear child!' She put her hand on Kate's shoulder, briefly, and then she and the orderly left her alone with Fred.

Kate hardly heard what she'd said; hardly noticed her going. She stroked Fred's cheek and his eyelids opened. For a second there was a glimmer of light in his eyes, almost a smile, and then he closed them again and drifted into a peaceful sleep. Kate stayed there with him all night, holding his hand until he died.

It was dawn by then. When Kate returned to the sleeping quarters, the members of the company were packing their things onto the truck, preparing to leave for the next camp, the next brave show. All the travelling was back towards Boulogne now, back towards home. Rowena had packed Kate's bag for her, and helped her up into the van.

'Are you all right, Kate?' Donald asked gently. 'Ready to move on?'

She smiled at him weakly. 'Yes,' she said. 'I'm ready.'

She leaned back against the seat as the driver started the engine and the vehicle made its bumpy way along the rutted track. The others had their eyes closed, weary with everything they had seen. She stared ahead blankly, seeing nothing except Fred's gaunt face; hearing nothing but the rasp of his breath as he had tried to sing with her. She opened her case and took out her writing pad.

'Dear Sadie', she wrote. She paused for a long time. She had so much to tell her sister, but she didn't have the words. Everything that she had experienced in the last few weeks felt as if it had been compressed into those last few moments with Fred. What was there to say, and how could she possibly say it?

I saw Fred Sweeney. He died last night. So sad. He was a nice young man.

Piercing the Veil

by Anne Fine

Piercing the Veil

They were beginning to become a little testy with one another, Alice could tell. Of course, their manners stayed perfect. Nobody thumped the table to make the shining cutlery dance or the wax spill in torrents down the candlesticks onto the damask cloth. Nobody leaned too far across their fruit plate, keen to make a point.

Still, they were arguing, and arguing hard.

'It is a nonsense! And a dangerous nonsense too,' declared her father.

'If it's such nonsense,' Mrs Parry said, 'how can it be dangerous? Mrs Short clearly believes she heard her dead son's voice while she was in the garden, and she feels comforted. Where is the harm in that?'

'False thoughts lead those who suffer down the wrong path,' insisted Alice's father. He ran an irritated finger round his stiff, white clerical collar as if to draw attention to the added weight of his opinion in the matter. 'The only proper comfort lies in true Christian belief. And we, as Christians, do not believe our dead can speak to us, the living, from beyond the grave.'

Mrs Parry persisted. 'But grief's such a stony, hopeless path. What does it matter if a few sad mothers find some ray of hope in trying to get in touch with the sons they've lost?'

Alice's father would have none of it. 'Bah! Table rapping! Talking to the dead! It's all a cheat, and a cruel cheat at that. This sudden plague of "spiritualists" are vultures preying on bruised souls.'

Such confidence! As usual Alice found herself lowering her head as if to protect herself from the sheer force of his conviction. Had her father put aside all doubts the day he was ordained a minister? Did he never think he might, for once, be *wrong*?

She trembled as his tone became more adamant. 'Liars and charlatans! I'd have them fiercely drummed out of each house they enter!'

Now grizzled Mr Pew opened his mouth for the first time. 'Perhaps,' he said, 'there has been too much fierce drumming over these last few months . . . '

They all fell silent, thinking of recent battles and the ever-lengthening lists of dead. The words 'Missing in Action' seemed to be heard more often than the tolling bells. Alice recalled a school assembly only a few days before. There stood the pupils in their perfect rows while Mr Abbot read the names of boys who'd fallen in these last desperate autumn weeks of warfare. Most eyes stayed fixed on the floor. But Alice had glanced up and been astonished to see that, though Mr Abbot's voice was barely faltering, tears rolled down his face. How odd! For all the village knew that, at the sale of work in aid of comforts for the troops, Lady Gilmond had given the most rousing speech, 'while still crumpled in her hand,' Mrs Parry said admiringly, 'she had the very telegram that she'd been given less than ten minutes before, informing her that her beloved Edward had died of wounds.'

Was Lady Gilmond stronger in the face of loss than Mr Abbot was with news of boys he'd only taught? Or had she gone home to weep as bitterly as Alice had when her own mother died? It was so hard to tell what people felt. Everyone was determined not to undermine the resolve of all those men on crowded troop trains trundling day and night through Alderley Junction. And more and more of them seemed to be on their way to the front.

Two nights before, she'd heard her father stifle a bark of astonishment as he read his newspaper. From where she sat, hopelessly fishing for yet another slipped stitch in the sock she was knitting for some soldier she would never meet, Alice took care to note the page. What had the Reverend Milner seen? The name of yet another man or boy he'd known? News of a further scrimping of the rations?

As soon as he had left the room, she'd hurried over to scour the dense print. So far as she could tell, the only thing that could have caused his surprise was yet another slackening of the height rules for enlisted men. Now they were happy to make soldiers of those they would have spurned when this long war began.

For such a change to have been made, how many must have fallen in between?

Fallen ... Mr Pew never failed to scowl each time he heard her say the word. 'Fallen, indeed, Elise! More likely shot to pieces!' (He was the only one to stick to her baptismal name after her father had so tactfully ushered in that tiny switch of sounds that turned the Germanic-sounding 'Elise' into the English 'Alice'.)

And he was scowling over their table now. 'Vicar, you rail so passionately against these mediums and fakers. But you must admit that, if men talked more on this earth, no one would need to try to talk to those who've been blown out of it fifty years too soon!'

'Hush!' scolded Mrs Parry. She waved a warning hand in Alice's direction. 'Now we must thank this young lady for her delicious contribution to our meal, and let her get back to her handiwork.'

Alice took this for what it was – a firm dismissal. But though the three of them might make her leave the room, they couldn't stop her wondering. She'd never for a moment thought the restless dead returned to comfort those they'd left behind, and give them messages. Just like her father, she believed that was a nonsense. But Mrs Short had been so sure that she'd heard Peter's voice behind her in the garden that she was not the least surprised to get the letter from the War Office. *'It is my painful duty to inform you ... '*

'Do *you* believe it?' Alice had dared ask her friend Hannah. 'Do you believe your mother truly heard your brother speak?'

Hannah had said no more than, 'She swears it's true.'

But Alice's father had explained, 'Mrs Short is a mother. These women are consumed with terrors for their beloved sons. Their minds are partially unhinged, their imaginations aflame. Small wonder that they see and hear things that aren't there.'

And yet . . . And yet . . .

For next time Alice had gone to see her friend, Hannah slipped into the room where Mrs Short was sleeping away her grief and took the letter that had come from Peter's commanding officer. Proudly she showed it to Alice, and with good reason, for the letter spoke of what a fine young man Peter had been, and how his fellow soldiers loved and trusted him, how brave he was, how quick and painless his death.

Then Alice felt the coldest shiver down her spine. 'But here the Colonel says it happened in the dawn attack on the eighteenth.'

Hannah took back the letter, carefully refolding it along creased lines. 'It was a mighty battle,' she confided. 'My uncle was in Dover. He came home saying he had heard the rumble of the guns across the Channel all day.'

Alice persisted. 'But the eighteenth is when your mother heard your brother's voice! And I remember that because you came to tell me as I was laying out the marrows for our Harvest Festival.'

Hannah looked up. 'What better evening to come and speak to her?'

So easy to believe! But Alice could almost hear the scathing words her father would have had to force himself not to say: 'What better evening to *imagine* it, after she had been told the bloody barrage had gone on for hours?'

She only said to Hannah, 'So you do truly believe that the dead can return?'

Now Hannah was embarrassed. But bravely she told her friend, 'I have no reason to doubt it. And Mother's not the only one. Ask Mrs Gregory.'

'From Wendle Post Office?'

'Yes. Both her sons were killed on the same day. She was bereft. But then a friend invited her to meet a lady in London. "She has the gift," she told Mrs Gregory. "This lady can pierce the veil between this world and the next." So Mrs Gregory took the train and went to the lady's house. She was called Marie-Claire, and Mrs Gregory said she welcomed her as if they were old friends, and pressed her to a reviving glass of sherry after her journey. Then two more strangers joined them. One was a man whose daughter had died two months before. He didn't speak about it, but Marie-Claire whispered to Mrs Gregory that there had been an explosion in a shell factory and her poor body was never found. The other visitor was a mother like herself.'

'What did they do?'

'It was so simple. They all sat round a little wooden table, "For all the world," said Mrs Gregory, "as if we were about to play a hand of bridge." They laid their palms flat with their fingers spread to form a circle, and Marie-Claire warned them that it was most important not to pull away. She said the energy ran round the ring of hands and mustn't be broken or it might tug her over onto the wrong side.'

'The wrong side?'

'Through the veil of death into the other world.'

Again the shiver ran down Alice's back. Could it be possible? Then death would seem so much less black. Why, Alice might even get to see her own dear mother again! Hear that soft voice! Feel those warm, comforting arms – and, for the first time ever, see that look of grim certainty drop from her father's face.

Keenly, she asked her friend, 'What happened next? Did Mrs Gregory say?'

Hannah took up the story. 'She told my mother that they all sat quietly for a while. The man who'd lost his daughter was weeping soundlessly, but couldn't brush away his tears for fear of breaking the circle. And Mrs Gregory admitted that though her heart went out to him as someone in as much anguish as herself, still she was thinking herself a fool to have gone all the way to London to see and hear nothing. Then there was a knock.'

'A knock?'

'A sharp rap on the table. But no one's hands had moved – no, not one inch, said Mrs Gregory. Marie-Claire threw back her head and asked, "Who has come back to us? Make yourself known." And instantly there came a strange rustling

ANNE FINE

sound. Mrs Gregory insisted that all the hands were in plain sight and never moved. And yet this rustling noise spread out from Marie-Claire, "As if," she told my mother, "all manner of tiny spirits might be whispering."'

Alice had heard her father ranting on about 'these charlatans' often enough to feel obliged to say, 'Perhaps her petticoats...? Or something clever tucked inside her bodice?'

'Perhaps. But then she told the father that his daughter sent her love and urged him not to grieve because her pain was over. Only happiness had greeted her in her new place and she was not alone; she'd met her aunt. The man looked puzzled and said, "My daughter has no aunts!" Then he thought a moment and said, "Wait! That would be her godmother. My daughter always called her 'aunt' – and she passed over only a year ago." Marie-Claire smiled and told him that "the recently translated", as she called them, were often first to comfort newcomers. And, anyway, in that strange other world to come, relationships often seem hazy.'

Once again Alice could imagine her father's contemptuous snort. 'Oh, how convenient!'

But, curious, she asked her friend, 'So was the poor man satisfied?'

'Satisfied?'

'That it was not some trickery, like my father says.'

She'd touched a sore spot. Hannah's eyes flashed. 'And does your father also say my mother is mistaken in recognising Peter's voice?'

Alice could only say, 'My father's bound to question anything that doesn't fit with his beliefs.'

'So he could never see a spirit plain if it stood right beside him!'

Alice put out a soothing hand. 'Finish your story about Mrs Gregory. Was there a message from her boys?'

'No, not that day. But she is going back. And she is filled with hope.'

Hope. Was it an accident her father took this as the theme for his next sermon? He climbed the steps into his high, carved pulpit and took a moment to survey the scattering of black hats and silvered heads. He said, 'My text is from the book of Romans: "Rejoicing in hope; patient in tribulation".' To Alice, as she drifted off into her own thoughts, it seemed the usual weave of exhortation and reproach: '"Hope" in the Bible is not what we mean when we say we "hope" that the fine weather will hold or that our bread dough will rise. No, it means "trust". When we hope in the Lord, we trust in him completely. We know he cares about the tiniest thing that happens to every one of us, and so...'

Only a pew or two behind her, Alice could hear odd, sharp intakes of breath. Was someone stifling tears? She dared not turn to look – not with her father looming above them, running his fingertips along the edge of the pulpit in that nervous habit which only stopped when he at last bowed his head and, in the deeper voice he used for prayer, signalled the end of his sermon. 'In the name of the Father...'

Now she could turn.

It was Mrs Coral.

Oh, please no! Not her son too! Not big, soft, gentle Sam!

The small black heap of misery was slumped in the pew beside Mrs Parry's housekeeper. They were the only two women left to serve in The Lodge now that the younger maids had gone to work in factories, or on the land. Her face was grim and her nose raw from dabbing. She barely could be recognised as the kind, capable woman Mrs Parry had sent across the village to watch over Alice's mother through those last, long, sad nights. More than once Alice had woken with a start of dread, and padded down the icy corridor to be so calmly comforted and then led back to bed by Mrs Coral.

She loved the woman, so she couldn't stop herself. As soon as her father had dismissed his flock with the blessing, she hurried down the aisle to clutch at Mrs Coral's companion's arm. 'Is it..?'

Mrs Parry's housekeeper turned. 'Sam, yes.'

'I am so very sorry.'

The dark eyes narrowed and the words were spat. 'Ah, well. We must all do what Reverend Milner orders us, mustn't we? We must just *trust*.'

The force of it was such a shock that Alice stumbled back. How could this woman beside poor Mrs Coral show such contempt for what her father believed? And in his own church too!

She was so keen to get away, but Mrs Parry was behind her. 'Alice, the socks and comforters you've knitted for the sale of work – when will you bring them?'

Oh, when indeed! For none of them were finished. She'd started with such determination. (Those poor men in those sodden, flooded trenches! The socks rotting on their feet!) But she had slipped so many stitches that she'd been ashamed, and unravelled everything. She stammered out a feeble answer, though she knew there was very little chance of having anything to show before the end of the week. Her lack of skill was mortifying. In these bad times, everyone did what they could. Old men dug vegetable gardens and mended everything from fishing reels to fences. None of the women let a moment pass without reaching for their wool or sewing baskets. As for her father, he walked miles every day, from one house to another, attempting to console the endless stream of freshly widowed women and grieving families. And Alice's own mother, had she lived, would have been following in his wake with what small comforts she herself could bring.

Everyone played their part. Everyone.

Except for Alice.

What could she do? Too clumsy with the needles to make anything fit to sell or send. Too young to go to work, too old to stay oblivious to all the efforts round her. Why, even these 'spiritualists' her father so despised for trickery on those they preyed upon, did something useful.

They brought hope to others.

But Alice could at least offer to Mrs Coral the same plain human sympathy the woman had shown her when she had lost her mother. She hurried after as the pair started down the lane. Affecting to ignore a further hostile look from the sharp-tongued companion, Alice begged, 'Please, Mrs Coral! Say I may come to sit with you one evening soon.'

The woman was too steeped in grief to answer. She could not even shake her head before she was firmly pulled away.

But she had not said no.

A vicarage is a busy place when death is all about. It was a week before Alice tapped on the back door of The Lodge. With some relief she learned the fierce housekeeper was out and Mrs Parry had already gone to bed, pleading an aching head. Alice stoked up the dying kitchen fire to which Mrs Coral had seemed indifferent. The two sat quietly for a while as shadows loomed and danced, and rain beat on the window. Then Alice spoke of how, when she was little more than eight or nine years old, Sam tied his handkerchief around her bleeding knee and carried her home.

His mother stirred on her small chair. 'My Sam was a precious gift. Child, boy and man, I never knew him say a mean word or do a spiteful thing.'

In her head Alice heard the echo of something her father often said when he came back from funerals: 'The day they die, all men turn into saints!' Everyone knew Sam had his faults. There was talk of his poaching, and he was never seen in church – indeed, the day he'd carried Alice home, he'd grinned as he walked past it, calling it 'The House of Fairy Tales'. But suddenly Alice saw her father's words for what they were – hard and contemptuous. How could a man of God be so quick to dismiss the feelings of people he knew well? Had steely righteousness sucked all the kindness from his soul? Could nothing pierce the veil of his assurance? To her astonishment, as Mrs Coral sat remembering the sweetness and goodness of her son and let herself forget the rest, Alice began to feel resentment rising inside her at her father's stubborn lack of charity.

After a while the strain of talking of the boy she'd lost became too much for Mrs Coral. Dabbing her eyes, she turned the conversation to the vicarage. So Alice spoke of how her mother's room had now become her own, and how, in the neglected garden, she hoped some day to tell a valued plant from a rank weed. Mrs Coral made every effort to show interest. But grief drains all the meaning from other people's lives, and Alice knew that nothing she could think to say was likely to distract or console her.

Except...

Was it the force of feeling against her father's lack of kindness that empowered her? How else, she asked herself afterwards, could someone raised in the shadow of the pulpit dare take advantage of a foolish tale heard only a short time before? For suddenly Alice was determined to offer Mrs Coral something far more comforting than any words she might hear from the minister's lips.

She interrupted her own talk of efforts in the garden to say,

'That noise. Did you hear it?'

'What noise, my dear?'

'That tread behind the door.'

'Perhaps Mrs Parry...?'

'No,' Alice said. 'It was a man's firm footsteps.'

Mrs Coral shook her head. 'But I heard nothing.'

'It must be my imagination.' Alice took up her tale about cutting the wrong shoots on the raspberry canes, then stopped again. 'Surely you heard it this time? That creak as the door opened. That must have caught your ear.'

'No, Alice. All I hear is rain and wind.'

'But I could swear— Yes! There it is again. And closer! He is in the room with us!'

'He?'

Alice forced her eyes into the roundness of astonishment. 'You don't feel anything? You don't feel – how can I say it best? – as if there were *another* in the room?'

Mrs Coral gathered her shawl more tightly round her. 'Another, Alice?'

Alice said wonderingly, as if confused, 'Not quite a person, no – but some sort of presence.'

'A *presence*?' She could see Mrs Coral tremble at the thought. 'Some sort of spirit?'

'If it's a spirit,' Alice declared, 'then it's a kind one, for I never had a feeling of such warmth and love steal over me out of nowhere.'

She watched the drawn, pinched face in front of her. She saw hope spring. And Alice knew that she had led poor Mrs

Coral to the point of saying it herself: 'Then it's my Sam come back! You see him and I don't!'

'I don't quite *see* him,' Alice said. She pressed a finger to her brow and took a chance. 'You know my mother always said I had a strange way of sensing things that aren't there. But all our visitor is to me right now is shadow.' She pointed above Mrs Coral's head. 'There. Between you and the door.'

Mrs Coral swung round. 'No! I see nothing!'

'You *feel* it, surely, though? A kind and comforting presence?' She watched as Mrs Coral turned back in the fireside chair and closed her eyes. 'And he's stepped closer now. He's still a shadow, but he smiles and stretches out a hand to touch you.'

'Alice, I think I feel it on my shoulder! Yes, I am sure I do!'

Alice thought back to Marie-Claire and Mrs Gregory. 'He wants to tell you something. I don't know how I know this, but I do. He wants to tell you that he's safe and happy now. No pain can touch him. You must not be troubled. And he'll watch over you until you join him.'

'Oh, Alice! Tell him to pray that day will come soon!'

That was a step too far.

'He can't do that. That would be very wrong.' But what had she heard her father saying once, over a tiny baby's grave? Oh, yes! 'Sam wants to tell you that some lives are meant to be long and others short. But any life that has been lived in God's good grace is a life lived to the full.'

She watched a tear roll down the old, lined face. She watched the wrinkled fingers relax and spread on the worn arm of the chair.

'And,' Alice said, 'he wants to tell you he'll be back to comfort you. You'll know whenever he's there, and you'll know what he wants to say to you.'

'Tell him...' Mrs Coral threw out her hands. 'Oh, Alice! Tell him...'

'I can't,' said Alice simply. 'Because he's gone.'

It was a chilly walk back to the vicarage but Alice shivered from far more than cold night air. She felt herself poisoned with guilt. The spirits of dead people did not return to comfort those they'd left behind. The idea was a nonsense, and Alice had deliberately turned herself into one of those very cheats her father railed against. She had deceived and lied, and offered false assurance to one of his flock. What had he called such people? Vultures preying on bruised souls? Should she be drummed out too?

But then – perhaps Sam had been right! Perhaps the church's beliefs were no more than fairy tales of a different kind. It was so hard, these days, to think there truly was a loving God. Perhaps her father was deceived as well! Perhaps she was no worse than him in the false comfort she had tried to offer.

She had no fear her father would be told what she had done. The next day Mrs Coral was to travel to Hove to spend a few weeks with her sister. And Mrs Coral knew the

Reverend Milner well enough to understand Alice's plea for secrecy. She wouldn't say a word.

Still, Alice told herself she would regret what she had done for ever. She crept home through the shadows like the sinner that she feared she was, and tiptoed up the stairs as quietly as she could.

Her father was the last man she could face on such a night.

The weeks passed. News from the War stayed grim, and though in school assemblies Mr Abbot still had the dismal task of reading out the names of boys he'd taught, now only the sombre look on his face gave any hint of feeling. At home in the vicarage, the dark winter evenings dragged on so long that even Alice's clumsy handiwork had time to improve. Soon it was rare for her to drop a stitch, even when turning awkward sock heels, and Mrs Parry began to praise her. 'Such fine work, Alice! Your poor dead mother would be proud of you.'

Of Mrs Coral there had been no sign, and Alice was relieved to hear she was still with her sister. She had no wish to see the face that would refresh the surge of guilt she felt each time she thought of what she'd done that night.

The year turned. Up in the pulpit Reverend Milner spoke again about the lowering nature of despair. He would not call it a sin. 'No. After all, the body and the mind can take only so much before our courage falters. But from the dark lair of despondency, we must all trust that one day...'

Was Alice listening? No, she was not. Because, turning her head to watch the morning light gleam through stained glass, she'd spotted in the furthest row a carefully trimmed hat she thought she recognised.

Mrs Coral was back. But she was barely recognisable once again. This time her face was lifted and her eyes were bright. Her cheeks had filled out, and those restless fingers now lay in peace on her prayer book. Even as Alice stared, Mrs Coral turned her head and gave her the warmest smile.

Alice could barely wait until the service ended. They met beyond the gate, where Mrs Coral waited arm in arm with her companion from The Lodge.

'You look so well!' said Alice.

'And I hear such good things of you, my dear! If you heard Mrs Parry praising your handiwork, your ears would burn. So will you come one evening to tell us all your news?'

'As soon as I can.'

They parted with a hug, and Mrs Coral hurried off to greet another friend. But her companion stayed behind to catch at Alice's arm. 'Alice, I hope you understand exactly what you did that night.'

Alice flushed hot with shame and stared at her boots. Now she would be exposed! What would her father say when he was told? Would he disown her for ever or, worse, weep at his failures both as a father and a minister?

The housekeeper kept her hand on Alice's arm. 'You know she talks to Sam now? All the time. She says he's with her often and she swears that he speaks back to her.'

Alice looked up. But where was the grim and hostile look that she remembered all too well? The woman's face had softened into a smile. 'Well may your father preach from his lofty pulpit about the virtues of trust. But you, my dear, were brave enough to step out on a rainy night and offer *real* hope.'

The words fell like forgiveness. Alice felt her misery and guilt fading away. So hope had two meanings after all! One for her father, one for her. And his was his – to do with learning and convictions. And hers was hers – to do with friendship and with love.

As Mrs Parry's housekeeper leaned closer to squeeze the young girl's arm, she added one last blessing. 'And surely hope is worth a hundred thousand pairs of knitted socks.'

The Green Behind the Glass

the Glass

by Adèle Geras

The Green Behind the Glass

1916, November

The telegram was addressed to Enid. Sarah put it carefully on the table in the hall. The white envelope turned red in the light that fell through the coloured squares of glass above the front door. She had no desire to open it. She knew that Philip was dead. The possibility that he might be wounded, missing in action, captured, never occurred to her. It was a death she had been expecting; these were only the official words setting it out in writing. For a moment, Sarah wondered about the people whose work it was every day to compose such messages. Perhaps they grew used to it. The telegraph boy, though, couldn't meet her eyes.

'Telegram for Miss Enid Romney,' he'd said.

'I'll take it. I'm her sister. They're all out.'

'Much obliged, I'm sure.' He had thrust the envelope into her hand and run towards the gate without looking back, his boots clattering along the path. The envelope had fluttered suddenly in a rush of wind.

Sarah sat on the oak settle in the hall and wondered

whether to take the message to Enid in the shop at once. To them, she thought, to the writers of this telegram, Philip is Enid's young man. He was. Was. Haven't we been preparing for the wedding, embroidering and stitching since before the War?

It seemed to Sarah that they'd always known Philip Stansforth. The two families, Stansforths and Romneys, had been neighbours in the days before Sarah's father died. She was five when that had happened and she had little memory of him, recalling only a big, jolly presence, a round, smiling face and a very tickly moustache. Mother and Sarah and Enid had had to fend for themselves as best they could. They had sold the big house in Kentish Town and moved south of the river, so that Mother could work in a draper's shop run by her elderly cousin, Maudie.

Philip and his mama came often to visit. He was the same age as Enid, and four years older than Sarah. Looking back now, she couldn't remember a time when she didn't adore him. She used to pretend that he was her brother. Enid did her very best to leave Sarah out of their activities, but Philip didn't seem to mind her being there. He made sure to include her in card games and even let her help with the putting-together of huge and intricate jigsaw puzzles. How we used to love those, Sarah thought. When did we stop doing them? The pieces would be spread out all over the table in the dining room. Somehow she always managed to sit next to Philip and find just the right pieces to go in the bits that he was working on.

'Clever Sarah,' he'd say and smile at her fondly. 'That's just the bit of sky I need. I must say, you've got a very good eye for these puzzles.'

Enid always sat up straighter when Philip praised her sister and tried not to look put out, but Sarah could see that she was vexed.

It was Mother and Mrs Stansforth between them who encouraged the engagement. As Philip and Enid grew older, Sarah was urged to leave them to their own devices more and more. They began to walk out together, to visit museums and parks, and take tea in local teashops. Sarah was still at school. By the time she was fourteen and left to work in the shop with Mother, it was too late. Enid was eighteen and so was Philip, and neither of them could imagine, it seemed, a life different from the one which had been suggested to them.

When the engagement was first announced, Sarah was as happy as everyone else and began to look forward to a wedding day and a bridal dress. But the years passed and the wedding ceased to be mentioned. It seemed to Sarah as though 'being betrothed' must be a state so comfortable and respectable in itself that you didn't need to concern yourself with the business of actually getting married.

And then War had been declared.

Sarah stood up and looked at herself in the mirror that hung above the settle. She saw straight, fair hair, tied back; eyes which were not exactly blue (Philip called them 'sea-coloured'); a small mouth and a pale complexion. Am I pretty? she asked her reflection. Philip thought so. The day he told her was when she first realized she was in love with him, though to be truthful she couldn't remember a single hour when she hadn't loved him. The only thing that changed was the quality of that love; the way it made her feel.

They had met in the street. Philip had just got off the omnibus (he was coming to visit Enid), and Sarah was on her way home from the shop. Of course they walked together – why would they not? They were going to be related soon enough. Part of the same family.

'You're not a little girl any longer, are you?' Philip said. He said it suddenly, right in the midst of their conversation, interrupting himself.

'No,' Sarah said. 'I'm sixteen.'

'You're very pretty, Sarah,' he said. He put out his hand and took hers. They were standing in the shadow of the hedge, just a few houses down from where Enid was waiting for him. He pulled her towards him and before Sarah could find words to object, he was kissing her: hard, passionately, on the mouth, as she had never been kissed before. She nearly swooned from the strangeness and unexpectedness of it. How long did it last? Two seconds? Three? Maybe minutes? She had no idea. She knew only that her whole body seemed to turn a kind of somersault, lurching and falling and melting. Then just as suddenly Philip pulled away. 'I'm sorry,' he said. 'I've behaved like a cad. I should never have kissed you. Please forgive me and promise me that this . . . will be our secret. Do you promise?'

Sarah had nodded, overcome. And she had kept her word. It should have ended there. But whenever she saw Philip (and that was often) the memory of the kiss seemed to hang between them and Sarah would imagine it happening again and again. She could see that Philip felt it too. Something like an electrical charge passed between them, unguessed at by anyone else.

Sarah's eyes fell to the telegram. Enid will enjoy mourning, she thought. She will look elegant in black. She'll cry delicately so as not to mar the whiteness of her skin and she'll dab her nose with a lace-edged handkerchief. All the customers will sigh and say how sad it is, and young men will want to comfort and console her, and they will succeed, oh yes, because she didn't really love him.

'She didn't really love him!' Sarah found herself saying the words aloud and blushed as if there were a part of Enid lurking somewhere that could overhear her. 'Not really,' she whispered. 'Not like I did.' I know, she thought, because she told me.

Enid is sewing. I ask her: 'Do you really love him, Enid? Does your heart beat so loudly sometimes that you feel the whole world can hear it? Can you bear it, the thought of him going away? Do you see him in your dreams?'

'Silly goose! You're just a child!' She smiles at me. She is grown up. Her face is calm. Pale. 'And you've been reading

too many novels. I respect him. I admire him. I am very fond of him. He is a steady young man. And besides, ladies in real life don't feel those things. It wouldn't be right.'

But I felt them, thought Sarah. And other feelings too, which made me blush. I turned away, I remember, so that Enid would not see my face, and thought of his arms holding me, and his hands in my hair and his mouth . . . oh, such a melting; a melting in my stomach. *I* loved him. And I can never say anything. I shall only be able to weep for him at night, after Enid has fallen asleep. And I shall have to look at him. Enid will keep his photograph between our beds, the one that isn't him at all, just a soldier in uniform, sepia, like all the soldiers. Perhaps she will put it in a black frame, but after a while, I will be the only one who really sees it. I will look at it even though it's nothing like the Philip I know, because it is the only image of him that I have.

Sarah tried to cry and no tears would come. It seemed to her that her heart had been crushed in metal hands, icy cold and shining. How could she bear the tight pain of those hands? But soon, yes, she would have to pick up the telegram and walk to the shop and watch Enid fainting and Mother rustling out from behind the counter. Mrs Feathers would be there – she was always there – and she would tell, as she had told so often, the remarkable story of her Jimmy, who'd been posted as dead last December and who, six months later, had simply walked into the house, bold as you please, and asked for a cup of tea.

'You're mine now,' Sarah said aloud to the telegram. She giggled. Maybe I'm going mad, she thought. Isn't talking to yourself the first sign? I don't care. I don't care if I am mad. I shall go and change into my blue dress, just for a little while. Later, I shall have to wear mourning, Philip, even though I promised you I wouldn't. Mother will make me. What would the neighbours think otherwise?

'Philip is like a son to me,' Mother used to say, long before he proposed to Enid, 'one of the family.' She and Philip's mother would congratulate one another on the forthcoming marriage. They'd arranged the whole thing. She is good at arranging. Enid is piqued, sometimes, by the attention Philip pays me. I am scarcely more than a child. Mother says: 'But of course he loves Sarah too. Isn't she like a little sister to him?' When she says this, I clench my fists until the nails cut into my palms. I don't want that kind of love, no, not that kind at all.

Sarah laid the blue dress on the bed. The sun shone steadily outside, but the leaves had gone. Swiftly, she pulled the hatbox from under the bed, and lifted out the straw hat with the red satin ribbons. It had been wrapped in tissue paper, like a treasure. It was a hat for long days of blue sky, green trees and roses. I can't wear it in November, she thought. She had looked at it often, remembering the afternoon at Kew Gardens, so long ago, a whole three months. She had thought of this as the happiest day of her life, a day with only the smallest shadow upon it, the slightest wisp of fear, nothing significant to disturb the joy. But now Philip was dead, that short-lived moment of terror spread through her beautiful memories like ink stirred into clear water.

Enid's sewing-basket was on the chest of drawers. Sarah was seized suddenly with rage at Philip for dying, for leaving her behind in the world. She took the dress-making scissors out of the basket, and cut and cut into the brim of the hat until it hung in strips, like a fringe. She laid the ribbons beside her on the bed and crushed the crown in her hands until the sharp pieces of broken straw pricked her, hurt her. Then she snipped the long, long strips of satin into tiny squares. They glittered on the counterpane like drops of blood. When she had finished, her whole body throbbed, ached, was raw, as if she had been cutting up small pieces of herself. She lay back on the bed, breathless. I must go to the shop, she told herself. In a little while. If I close my eyes I can see him. I can hear his voice. And Enid's voice. Her voice was so bossy, that day.

'You can't wear that hat,' Enid says. 'It's too grown-up.'

'I am grown up.' I dance round the kitchen table, twirling the hat on my hand, so that the ribbons fly out behind it. 'I shall be seventeen at Christmas, and it's just the hat for Kew.'

'I don't know why you're coming anyway,' says Enid.

'Because it's a lovely day and because I invited her,' Philip says. He is leaning against the door, smiling at me.

212

'Thank you, kind sir,' I sweep him a curtsey.

'A pleasure, fair lady,' he answers and bows gracefully.

'When will you two stop clowning?' Enid is vexed. 'You spoil her all the time. I've had my hat on for fully five minutes.'

'Then let us go,' he says and offers an arm to Enid and an arm to me.

In the street, Enid frowns. 'It's not proper. Walking along arm-in-arm . . . like costermongers.'

'Stuff and nonsense,' says Philip. 'It's very jolly. Why else do you suppose we have two arms?'

I laugh. Enid wrinkles her nose. When we arrive in Kew Gardens we walk along the paths until we reach a wooden bench. 'August is a silly time to come here.' There is complaint in her voice. She is sitting between me and Philip. 'The camellias are long since over, and I love them so much. Even the roses are past their best.' She shudders. 'I do dislike them when all the petals turn brown and flap about in that untidy way.'

'Let's go into the Glass House.' I jump up and stand in front of them.

Enid pretends to droop. 'Philip,' she sighs. 'You take her. I don't think I could bear to stand in that stifling place, among the drips and smells.'

Philip rises reluctantly, touches Enid's shoulder. 'What about you though?' he says. 'What will you do?'

'I shall sit here until you return.' Enid spreads her skirts a little. 'I shall look at all the ladies and enjoy the sunshine.'

'We'll be back soon,' I say, trying to keep my voice from betraying my excitement. I am going to be alone with him. Will I ever be alone with him again? Please, please, please, I say to myself, let the time be slow, don't let it go too quickly.

Philip and I walk in silence. I am afraid to talk, afraid to open my mouth in case all the dammed-up words of love that I am feeling flood out of it.

We stand outside the glass Temperate House for a moment, looking in at the dense green leaves pressing against the panes. A cloud passes over the sun, darkens the sky, and we are reflected in the green, Philip's face and mine, together. In the dark mirror we turn towards each other. I stare at his reflection because I dare not look at him, and for an instant, his face disappears, and the image is of a death's head grinning at me; a white skull, bones with no flesh, black sockets with no eyes. I can feel myself trembling. Quickly, I look at the real Philip. He is there. His skin is brown. He is alive. His eyes are smiling at me.

'What is it, Sarah? Why are you shaking?'

I try to laugh and a squeak comes from my lips. How to explain? 'I saw something,' I say. 'Reflected in the glass.'

'There's only you and me.'

'It was you and me but you ... you had turned into a skeleton.'

The sun is shining again. Philip's face is sad, shadows are in his eyes as he turns to look. I look too, and the skull has vanished. I let out a breath of relief.

'It's only me after all,' he says.

214

'But it was there. I saw it so clearly. Philip, please don't die.'

'I shan't,' he says, seriously, carefully. 'I shan't die. Don't be frightened. It was only a trick of the light.'

I believe him because I want to believe him. He takes my hand. 'Let's go in,' he says.

Inside the Temperate House, heat surrounds us like wet felt. Thickly about our heads, a velvety, glossy, spiky, tangled jungle adds to the moisture that hangs in the air. Leaves, fronds, ferns and creepers glisten, wet and hot, and the earth that covers their roots is black, warm. Drops of water trickle down the panes of glass. The smell of growing is everywhere, filling our nostrils with a kind of mist. We walk between the towering plants. No one else is here. A long staircase, wrought-iron painted white, spirals upwards, hides itself in green as it winds into the glass roof. Philip is still holding my hand, and I say nothing. I want him to hold it for ever. I want his hand to grow into mine. Why doesn't he speak to me? Usually we laugh and joke and talk so much that Enid is perpetually hushing us. Now he has nothing to say. I think, Perhaps he is angry. He wants to sit with Enid in the cool air. He is cross at having to come here with me when his time with her is so short. He is leaving tomorrow and I have parted them with my selfishness and my love. Tears cloud my eyes. I stumble, nearly falling. My hat drops to the ground. Philip's hand catches me round the waist. I clutch at his arm, and he holds me and does not let me go when I am upright. We stand, locked together.

'Sarah . . .' It is a whisper. 'Sarah, I must speak.' The hand *about my waist pulls me closer. I can feel the fingers spreading out, stroking me. He looks away. 'I can't marry Enid,' he says. 'It wouldn't be right.'*

'Why?' There are other words, but they will not come.

'I can't tell her,' he mutters. 'I've tried. I can't.' He looks at me. 'I shall write to her. It's a cowardly thing to do, but I cannot bear to face her, not yet. Not now... Sarah?'

'Yes?' I force myself to look up.

'Sarah, do you know' – his voice fades, disappears – 'my feelings? For you?'

My heart is choking me, beating in my throat. I nod.

Philip goes on: 'I...I don't know how to say it.' He looks over my head, cannot meet my eyes. He speaks, his voice rough with emotion. 'I've thought and thought about it, and I don't know how to say it.'

He draws me closer. I can feel the buttons of his jacket through my dress. I am going to faint. I am dissolving in the heat, turning into water. His arms are around me, enfolding me. His mouth is pressing down on my head, moving in my hair. Blindly, like a plant in search of light, I turn my face up, and his lips are there, on my lips, and my senses and my heart and my body, every part of me, all my love, everything is drawn into the sweetness of his mouth.

Later, we stand together, dazed, quivering. I can feel his kiss still, pouring through me.

'Philip, Philip.' I bury my head in his jacket. 'I love you. I've always loved you.' Half hoping he will not hear me.

He lifts my face in his fingers. 'And I love you, Sarah.

Sarah, I love you. I don't know how I've never said it before. How did I make such a mistake?'

I laugh. Everything is golden now. What has happened... what will happen... Enid... the rest of the world... nothing is important.

'I'm only a child,' I say, smiling, teasing.

'Oh, no,' he says. 'Not any longer. Not a child.' He kisses me again, softly. His fingers are on my hair, on my neck, touching and touching me. I have imagined it a thousand times and it was not like this. Wildly, I think of us growing here in this hothouse for ever, like two plants twined into one another, stems interlocked, leaves brushing... I move away from him.

'We must go back,' I say.

'Yes.' He takes my hat from the ground and puts it on my head.

'You must promise me,' he says, 'never to wear mourning.'

'Mourning?' What has mourning to do with such happiness?

'If I die...'

'You won't die, Philip.' I am myself again now. 'You said you wouldn't. I love you too much. You'll come back and we'll live happily ever after, love one another for ever, just like a prince and princess in a fairy tale.'

He laughs. 'Yes, yes, we will. We will be happy.'

Walking back together to Enid's bench, we make plans. He will write to me. He will send the letters to my friend Emily. I shall tell her everything. He will write to Enid. Not at once *but quite soon. We can see Enid now. She is waving at us. We wave back.*

'Remember that I love you,' Philip whispers when we are nearly, oh, nearly there. I cannot answer. Enid is too close. I sit on the bench beside her, dizzy with loving him.

'You've been away for ages,' she says. 'I was quite worried.'

Philip's voice, answering her, is light, full of laughter. 'There's such a lot to look at. A splendid place. You really should have come.'

I am amazed at him. I dare not open my mouth. Here, in the fresh air, I cannot look at her. The dreadfulness of what I am doing to her...what I am going to do to her, makes me feel ill. Will she forgive us? Will we have to elope? Emigrate? There will be time enough to worry when she finds out; when Philip tells her. Now, I cannot help my happiness curling through me like a vine. We set off again along the gravel path. I have to stop myself from skipping. I remember, briefly, the skeleton I saw reflected in the glass, and I laugh out loud at my childish fear. It was only a trick of the light, just as Philip had said. A trick of the light.

There are stone urns near the Temperate House and carved stone flowers set about their bases. A lady is sitting on a bench in the sunshine under a black silk parasol. The light makes jagged pools of colour in the inky taffeta of her skirts, and her hat is massed with ostrich feathers as black as plumes in a funeral procession. She turns to look at us as we go by and I see that her face is old: small pink lips lost in a network of wrinkles; eyes still blue, still young under a *pale, lined brow. Black gloves cover her hands, and I imagine them veined and stiff under the fabric. She smiles at me and I feel a sudden shock, a tremor of fear.*

'Good afternoon,' she says, and I know she's talking to me.

'Good afternoon,' I answer. Enid and Philip walk on, but it would be rude for me to ignore her.

The lady continues. 'What's your name, child?'

'Sarah Romney.'

'Look at me carefully, Sarah. Can you believe I was just like you? Oh, I used to run through the gardens here with ribbons flying from my hat . . . It all passes.'

I smile. What can I say in answer to that? 'I must catch up with my sister,' I murmur. 'Goodbye.'

Enid is saying, 'Forty years out of date, at least. Do you think she realizes how out of place she looks?'

'Poor old thing,' says Philip. 'all alone in the world.' He begins to whistle the tune of 'Mademoiselle from Armentières'. 'How would you like it?'

'I do not think,' says Enid, 'that mourning dress should be so showy . . . Ostrich feathers indeed! Mutton dressed as lamb.'

I look back at the old woman. I feel pity for her, but she does not hold my attention. I start to run across the grass as fast as I can. They are chasing me; yes, even Enid, dignity forgotten, is running and running. Philip puts his hand on my waist and twirls me round. I glance fearfully at Enid, but she is smiling at us like an indulgent mother.

We walk home in the dusk. I must leave him alone with

Enid at the gate. He kisses me goodbye on the cheek, like a brother, and I go indoors quickly. I am burning in the places where he touched me.

Sarah sat up. Slowly, like a sleepwalker, she gathered the torn, bruised straw and the scraps of ribbon from the bed and the floor and put them in the hatbox. When there is time, she thought, I shall burn them in the kitchen fire. She struggled into the blue dress and looked at herself in the mirror. What she saw was the face of a stranger who resembled her: mouth pulled out of shape, skin white, hair without colour. She fastened, carefully, the buttons on her cuffs. Her skin, all the soft surfaces of her body, felt raw, scraped, wounded. I am wounded all over, she thought, and went slowly downstairs. She put the telegram in her pocket and left the house.

Enid comes out from behind the counter. She says: 'What's the matter, Sarah? Are you ill? You look so white. Why are you wearing that thin dress?'

Mother is talking to Mrs Feathers. It is absorbing talk. I do not think they have seen me. I say nothing. I give the envelope to Enid. She tears it open; a ragged fumbling of her hands, not like her at all.

'It's Philip,' she says. 'Philip is dead.'

I watch, mesmerized, as she falls in a liquid movement to the ground. Mother appears, loosens her waistband, brings out smelling salts. She is weeping noisily.

Mrs Feathers says: 'I'll put the kettle on for a cup of tea. Plenty of sugar, that's the thing for shock.'

I envy my mother every tear she is shedding. I want to cry and cannot. The iron grip tightens round my heart.

1919, May

'I think James will come to call this afternoon.' Enid's fingers made pleats in the lilac skirt she was wearing.

Sarah said, 'Do you like him?'

Enid considered the question. The sisters were walking in Kew Gardens. Enid wanted to look at the camellias. 'Yes,' she said at last, 'he is a fine man.'

Sarah thought of James's solid body and long teeth, his black hair and the small brush of his moustache. Over the months, scars had slowly covered the sore places in her mind but sometimes, especially at Kew, the pain took her breath away. She should not, she knew, walk there so often, yet she did. She should have avoided the Temperate House, but she went there at every opportunity and stood beside the streaming panes with her eyes closed, willing herself to capture something. Her feelings when she had stood with Philip in the same spot had been so overpowering, had filled her with such sharp pleasure, that she always hoped that their ghosts – hers and Philip's – must still be lingering among the leaves.

Now, she looked at Enid. 'I think,' she said, 'that James will suit you very well.'

'He hasn't proposed to me yet,' Enid said placidly. 'Although I don't think it will be too long...' Her voice trailed away.

'Philip,' Sarah said (and the word felt strange in her mouth, an unfamiliar taste, like forgotten fruit), 'Philip would be pleased you are happy.'

'Do you think so, really?' Enid looked relieved. 'Of course I was heartbroken, heartbroken at his death. You remember? I fainted there and then on the floor of the shop. I shall never forget it.'

'Neither shall I,' said Sarah.

'His letters in the months before his death were quite different,' said Enid. 'Did I ever tell you?'

'No.'

'More formal. Veiled. For ever talking about an important matter which he would discuss on his next leave. Not so... devoted.'

Sarah tried to stop herself from feeling happy at this revelation. Enid went on: 'His last letter was particularly strange. He was going to tell me something, he said. He couldn't bear to wait another day, but then the letter finished in a scrawl, messy and rushed. I suppose they had to go and capture some hill or wood. I shall never know what it was.'

'It doesn't matter now,' said Sarah.

'But it *is* vexing,' Enid said. 'I should have liked to know.'

Part of Sarah longed to tell her, to tell her everything, but she said nothing. They walked on, in the direction of the Temperate House.

'I shall sit here,' Enid said. 'Will you sit with me, or walk on a little further? I'm tired and the view of the camellias is best from this bench.'

'I'll walk on,' Sarah said. 'I shan't be long.'

She left Enid and found herself following the same path that they'd taken, all three of them, on that last day with Philip. She was wearing a hat very like the one she'd cut to ribbons a couple of years ago. Her mother had asked what had happened to that hat so many times that Sarah replaced it as soon as she could, taking the money from her wages. At first, she hated wearing it, but now it gave her a kind of comfort, reminding her of happier times; reminding her of Philip. She could almost hear him whistling that song, 'Mademoiselle from Armentières'...

The woman sitting on the bench was thin, with grey hair pulled back into a loose bun. Sarah glanced at her as she walked by and was seized with the strongest feeling that she'd seen her somewhere. I know her, she thought. Or she reminds me of someone... Was she a customer in the shop? No, that wasn't it. Sarah could feel the woman staring after her; feel the force of a gaze on the back of her neck. When she reached the end of the path, she looked round. I must have been imagining it, she told herself. I'm being silly. Of course she's not looking at me. Still, there *was* something strange about the way the woman was dressed. Her skirt was much, much too short. Sarah could see her thin legs in pale stockings, uncovered from just below the knee, and feet in brown shoes. Her outfit was very unfeminine...

That's almost like a man's jacket, Sarah thought. The woman wasn't married, or at least she wasn't wearing a wedding ring. Sarah always noticed such things.

On the way back to Enid, she had to pass quite close to the woman on the bench. As she drew level, the woman spoke.

'Such a lovely day, my dear,' she said. 'Don't you think it's a nice day?'

Sarah almost lost her footing. *I know that voice. I know her. But who is she?* Her head was spinning and she felt dizzy.

'Yes,' she said. 'Lovely.'

'Your hat,' the lady said. 'I used to have a hat just like that, years ago.'

The woman's voice seemed to come and go: some of her words were audible and then there were times when the wind – it must have been the wind – blew them away like dead leaves before Sarah could catch them. She smiled nervously. 'I have to go back to my sister,' she said.

The woman smiled, nodded and said nothing – Sarah was quite sure of that.

When she got back to Enid, Sarah glanced back at the bench, but it was empty; the woman had gone. How had that happened? Surely she could not have disappeared entirely in the moments since she'd spoken to Sarah?

Later, on their way home, Sarah and Enid passed by the Temperate House.

'Are you going in today?' Enid asked.

'No,' said Sarah, 'I'll just look in for a moment.'

She approached the glass and stared at her reflection, with the darkness of the green behind it, and touched the ribbons that fell from the brim of her hat. Where were they? Where was her hat? She could see no sign of it, nor of the ribbons. The face she saw in the glass wasn't hers. It was too thin. Her hair was grey, pulled back in a bun and her jacket . . . like a man's, tailored.

Sarah shook her head, moved closer to the pane, and the image changed. She was herself again. There was her own face, still young. Her blue dress, her straw hat with its ribbons. She shivered. A trick of the light, that was all it had been. Only a trick of the light.

'I don't think,' she said to Enid as they walked out through the tall wrought-iron gates, 'I don't think I shall be coming to Kew for a very long time.'

Going Spare
by Sally Nicholls

Going Spare

When I was fourteen, I was short, plump, mousy-haired and shy. When I was fourteen, I thought this was everything important there was to know about me. It would be many years before I discovered that it wasn't.

It didn't help that my little sister and brother were small, curly-haired and adorable. I despised them, of course.

The three of us lived with my parents in a tiny flat in a big house on the edge of London. I shared a room with my sister, who was messy, noisy and had a habit of bursting into loud sobs at the slightest provocation. I shared the rest of the flat with my brother, who was messier, noisier and obsessed with anything that said, 'Pow! Pow! Pow! Pow! Nyyyyaaa! Boom!'

The year was 1977. Luke Skywalker still thought Darth Vader had killed his father. The Wombles were wombling free on Wimbledon Common and ABBA were celebrating their fifth number one in two years. My sister dreamed of being a backing dancer. My brother dreamed of being an X-Wing pilot.

Mostly, I dreamed of escaping.

The place I usually escaped to was the top-floor flat, which belonged to a lady called Miss Frobisher. Miss Frobisher was very old – at least seventy – and rather severe-looking. Her flat was half the size of ours, but it seemed much bigger. Everything in Miss Frobisher's flat was just so. You could put something down, and when you came back a week later it would be exactly where you'd left it. Miss Frobisher led a calm and ordered life, doing exactly as she pleased, exactly when she pleased. When I was fourteen, that was the closest I knew to heaven. I used to escape to her flat to play her piano, read her books and eat squashed-fly biscuits at her mahogany table and pretend to be making an afternoon visit like a character in a Jane Austen novel.

My sister and brother were a little scared of Miss Frobisher. She had a way of looking down her nose at them when they were being particularly riotous, which silenced even my brother.

'Why isn't she married?' my sister said. All the other grown-ups we knew were.

'She probably didn't have much choice,' said my mother. 'Lots of women didn't after the War. There weren't that many young men left.'

She meant the First World War. Not the one with the Spitfires.

'Really?' I said. I was surprised. I thought I knew all about the First World War. Boys dying in muddy fields in France. 'If I should die, think only this of me' and 'Dulce et decorum est, pro patria mori'. War memorials in market squares and the names of the dead on the walls of churches. I'd never thought about the women, except possibly the nurses, in war films, in long skirts and hats with crosses on them.

'Oh, yes,' my mother said. 'It was terribly sad, really. Two million spare women, there were. A whole generation of maiden aunts, wasn't it, George?'

George was my father. He grunted.

'They used to teach at my school,' she said, and I had an odd vision of my mother, being taught by two million maiden aunts. 'There was Miss Sullivan who taught French; terrifying woman. And Miss Phillips, who taught English. We used to put spiders in her desk drawer to make her scream.'

Two million leftover women. I tried to imagine it. I couldn't.

'What did they all do?' I asked my mother, but my sister was attempting to drown my brother in the kitchen sink, and her attention was wandering.

'Oh,' she said vaguely, drifting over to my sister. 'Not a lot.'

I went to see Miss Frobisher the next day after school. My parents had an agreement whereby I could practise my scales on her upright piano, in return for plant-watering and cat-sitting duties when she went on holiday. I despised the piano, and usually contrived to bang out several rounds of whatever I was supposed to be practising as loudly as possible, before going to drink tea and borrow books from Miss Frobisher's bookcases.

Miss Frobisher was small and wiry. She had short, sleek, grey hair and bright green eyes. Despite being about twice as old as my parents, she had about four times as much energy. She didn't have my brother and sister, of course.

As Miss Frobisher was pouring the tea, I asked her about the leftover women.

'Don't they teach you that in school?' she said.

'No,' I said. The First World War at school was almost entirely poets and poppies and dead archdukes. And trenches. For something calling itself a world war, most of it seemed to have happened in France. 'Really two million leftover women?'

'Well, it felt like a lot more if you were a girl of my class,' said Miss Frobisher. Miss Frobisher was posh. 'All of the boys I knew were officers, of course, and the thing about being an officer is that you are rather expected to lead the charge. Half the boys in my brother's year at Balliol never came back, if you can imagine that.'

I tried to imagine it. All those dead boys were depressing enough. The thought of being expected to find a boyfriend among the few who came back was hideous.

'Your poor brother,' I said instead, not wishing to sound heartless.

'Yes, it was rather dreadful,' Miss Frobisher said briskly. 'We lost two cousins and an uncle, and my sister Sylvia lost a boy she was awfully keen on. That was hard. Still, you get on with life, don't you? If anything, it was something of a party, those years after the War. All those young girls, desperate to put the War behind them; and the young men not quite able to believe they'd survived. I had my coming-out ball after the war, and you never saw so many people trying so hard to enjoy themselves. Poor ducks,' she added, somewhat as an afterthought.

A coming-out ball, I knew, was a sort of party wealthy girls had thrown for them to announce that they were old enough to marry.

'Did they still expect you to find a husband?' I asked.

Miss Frobisher said, 'Ha! Well, of course they did! What else would someone like me do? You must understand,' she added, very seriously, 'that my sister and I had never been expected to do anything except get married and run a house. The fact that we were now unlikely to find a husband was simply our misfortune and our parents'. But it was decided that we would have our seasons in London, and if and when we failed, we would stay at home and keep house for our ageing parents.'

'How old were you?' I asked.

Miss Frobisher considered the question.

'I was eighteen,' she said. 'Sylvia – she was the pretty one – she was twenty. Sylvia was really very lovely. We all thought she might well manage to find a husband. My brother Ralph was twenty-two. He was the sensible one.'

'And which one were you?'

Miss Frobisher gave a surprisingly wicked smile.

'Ah,' she said. 'I was trouble.'

Miss Frobisher being 'trouble' comforted me. Someone who was trouble, I felt, would surely find a way to avoid a future 'keeping house', whatever that meant.

'Was it dreadful?' I said. 'The coming-out ball?' It certainly *sounded* dreadful, the idea of dressing up and standing there, while boys wandered past and *judged* you . . . I shuddered.

'Not so very dreadful,' Miss Frobisher said. 'That ball was mostly family, and elderly neighbours we'd known for years, and a few of Ralph's friends from university to make up the numbers of men. And everyone was very nice to you, of course. Like a birthday party. No, we didn't really understand what had happened until we came to London. I remember one dance in particular, the first of the season. It was held in a hotel in St James's and, of course, Sylvia and I were particularly excited, because as far as we were concerned, this was the beginning of our new lives as young adults.

'We arrived late at the dance and did what one always does at these things, which is to look for people we knew; girls from school and family friends. We were so used to a world that was mostly female that at first I don't think we noticed that there were only women around us. At my coming-out ball, all of the women had stood together, and so had the men.

'I looked hopefully through the crowd to the room where the dancing was to be. I could hear music. Perhaps the boys were already dancing?

'Mother was talking to Aunt Vanessa. I caught Sylvia's eye and whispered, "Shall we go and dance?"

'She nodded. She too had been looking at the room with a slight frown. She began to push her way through the crowd. I followed with my cousin Lizzie, craning our necks to take in every detail.

'You must understand that this was not a terribly sophisticated affair. A party composed almost entirely of teenagers and their parents will always be an awkward occasion, no matter how expensive the ball gowns might be. A few years later, I would attend some really elegant parties, and would immediately recognise the difference. But at the time, I was eighteen. I was torn between admiration for the glitter of the thing, and embarrassment that the guests were simply slightly older versions of the girls I had been to school with.

'And then the slow realisation.

'There were no boys.

'The room was full of ball gowns; wonderful dresses in rose and turquoise and cream and buttercup silk. But no men. Was this dance for women only? But, no, it couldn't be, because Ralph had said that he would try to come later, once the concert he was attending had finished. Perhaps we should warn him that there'd been some mistake?

'But then, out of the sea of colour, there was a boy, tall and thin in black and white. And another beside him. And now, as we moved towards the ballroom, there was a third; a boy of about my own age or younger, shockingly one-armed. I'd seen wounded soldiers before, of course. Sylvia and I had taken them gift baskets last Christmas. But to see one here, at what should have been a fairytale ball, was a sharp reminder of everything we'd lost.

'It was a dreadful ball. We stood on the edges of the dance floor for a while, watching the few boys spinning manfully around the floor, hoping to be asked to dance. The room was hot and crowded and full of disappointment. A couple of girls were in tears. I didn't cry, but I was frightened. If this was what the season was going to be like, how could I ever expect to find a husband?

'When Ralph arrived at half past ten, Mother was mobbed by her friends, all looking for an introduction for their daughters. All the girls were desperate to dance with him, and so of course were we. What was the point of having a brother if he wasn't prepared to take you on a chivalrous once-around-the-room?

'As soon as we'd finished, other girls came forward, pressing for an introduction, girls who knew us, or Lizzie.

'Ralph was as shaken by the whole thing as we were. Ralph was friendly and easy-going, and while he certainly wasn't unattractive, he'd never been the object of so much attention before.

'"It wasn't *me* they wanted," he said afterwards. "They didn't even know me. I could have had four heads, and they'd still have wanted me."

'Some of the boys we knew loved all the attention they now attracted; Ralph hated it. He married a plain, timid little thing in the end. They were ridiculously happy, much to the irritation of all her friends.

Sylvia and I were quiet during the car ride home, which was unusual for us. I was glad she didn't want to talk. I wouldn't have known what to say.

'But for months afterwards, for that whole year, I carried this voice in my head: *What if, what if, what if? What if I don't find a husband? What if no one ever wants to marry me?*'

'I didn't have any other options, you see, besides marriage.

'Or I didn't think I had.'

'But did you really, honestly believe that?' I said. 'That no one would marry you? I mean, I could see you might worry about it. But surely you didn't give up hope *entirely*?'

'Sylvia didn't,' said Miss Frobisher. 'She was always very determined. But the thing was, there were so many other determined girls, and so few boys left.

'That first ball was the worst. But like all the other girls, we were beginning to realise that if we wanted to be married, we couldn't afford to pick or choose. Many of my friends ended up with husbands who were ten or twenty years older than they were. Some married men who were wounded, inside or out. Most of their marriages were happy enough, as far as I could tell. It became very fashionable to say that the best of our generation had died, but if I'm honest, I never saw that. And, after all, what about us girls? We were still here!

'Those two seasons after the War, when we were in London looking for husbands, were particularly hard for

Sylvia. Boys liked her – they always had – but they could sense her desperation, and that always makes a man hesitate. The boys would spend all evening flirting with Sylvia. She'd come home wound up and nervous, and then we'd stay up half the night in our hot little bedroom in the London house, while she asked over and over, "But *did* he like me? Do you think he really did?" And then a month or two later the boy in question would announce his engagement to the Honourable Miss So-and-So, and Sylvia would weep as though her heart was breaking. Sylvia's heart was broken an average of once a month. I tried to be sympathetic, but I confess that I couldn't help but be jealous. I didn't have the chance to get my heart broken. The only boys who ever deigned to dance with me were my cousins, or friends of Ralph, and then only out of politeness.'

'Poor Sylvia,' I said. 'What happened?'

Miss Frobisher smiled.

'Well,' she said. 'It was a funny thing. Christmas 1920 we spent with my aunt and uncle in the Lake District. Beautiful country. The local tarns froze over and we went skating every day. One morning we were out on the ice and Sylvia met a man. We didn't think too much of it at first, because she was always meeting men, but the next day we went skating again and there he was, and again the day after that. And then, a few weeks later, she came home bright-eyed and glowing, and announced that she was engaged to be married.

'I was in the front room, writing to our cousin Lizzie in London. Sylvia came dancing in, her cheeks pink with the cold.

'"Arthur proposed!" she said.

'"He did what?" I said.

'I admit that this isn't how one is supposed to respond when one's sister announces her engagement, but Arthur wasn't at all the sort of man I'd expected Sylvia to marry. He was a farmer's son, you see. That's how he'd escaped the War, working the land. A lot of the Lakeland men had stayed at home, farming or mining. Arthur Hepplewhite, his name was. But he seemed a nice chap. Quiet, respectful, with a thick north country accent, all short vowels and a long, hill-farmer's "Ehhh" when he was pleased about something.

'"Well!" said Sylvia. "You needn't make that sort of face. They may not have much money, but they're gentlemen farmers, you know."

'"You sound like Elizabeth Bennet," I told her. "Telling Lady Catherine de Bourgh that she's a gentleman's daughter and Mr Darcy is a gentleman."

'Sylvia and Arthur were a bit like Elizabeth and Darcy. Except that we weren't anywhere like as wealthy as Mr Darcy, and Arthur Hepplewhite's family were poorer even than the Bennets. True, Arthur had gone to a third-rate imitation public school in Carlisle. But when War was declared he'd left school early to assist his father with the farm work, and since then his life was spent helping with the lambing and the shearing, and searching for lost sheep in the fog.

"'He may be a gentleman," I said. "But he's not Father's sort of gentleman. Can you imagine him at Ascot? Or in London for the season?"

'Both Sylvia and I giggled, nervously. Arthur – with his flat cap and his hobnail boots – at Ascot!

"'I mean it, Sylvia," I said. "Do you think you could be happy as a farmer's wife?"

"'Yes," said Sylvia. She spoke plainly and directly. "I love Arthur. He's a good man, and I think we could make each other happy. And besides" – she sounded sad now – "it's not as though I have much choice, do I?"

'She got to her feet. "I need to talk to Father," she said. "I know Arthur should ask for my hand himself, but I don't want Father to be rude, and he will if I don't explain things first."

"'Father will say no," I said. Of course he would. I thought of the farmhouses we'd seen on the fells – low, whitewashed buildings, with walls two-foot-deep to keep out the cold. How, in heaven's name, could Sylvia believe she would be happy living in a place like that?

"'He won't," said Sylvia, but he did. He refused his consent outright. Mother wept, and so did I, but Sylvia stayed very calm, at least at first. We went to tell Arthur – who had been waiting patiently at the bottom of the garden.

'Then she wept, and Arthur put his arms around her shoulders, patted her back and muttered, "Eh, lass," and "I didn't mean to make all this trouble, now."

'He seemed to be addressing this last to me.

'"Oh no, of course you didn't. No one believes that," I said, like the well-brought-up young lady that I was, putting the servants at ease. He was a nice man, and handsome enough, if you liked that sort of thing.

'Days passed, and Mother worried, and our uncle tried to reason with Sylvia, and our cousins whispered in corners, and so did the servants, and at last Sylvia saw that this wouldn't do. She took Father away for a walk in the garden. They were away for hours, and when they came back, I saw that they'd both been crying. I think we young people forgot how hard the War had been for men like Father. He led half the men in our village into battle, and brought six back alive.

'"What did you say?" I asked her later, when we were getting ready for bed.

'"I told him that I'd tried doing things Mother's way and it hadn't worked," she said calmly, pulling the pins from her hair, "and that I had no intention of dying an old maid. I told him that Arthur loved me, and I thought I probably loved him, and at any rate, we both thought we could make the other happy. Isn't that the most important thing? I said that Arthur had been quite clear about what my life would be like and, no, it wasn't exactly the future I'd planned for myself, but it was a damn sight better than living at home as the unmarried daughter and running the Sunday School."

'After that there was no more fuss, and Sylvia and Arthur were married. They had six children, four boys and two girls, and all lived tumbled up together in a little white farmhouse on the fells. She's a grandmother eleven times over now. I don't think her life was always easy. But I think she was happy.'

'But what about you?' I said. 'What happened to you?' I hadn't forgotten that Miss Frobisher was the sister who was 'trouble'. I suspected that a girl who was trouble wouldn't just stay at home and look after her parents. I was half expecting to hear that she'd run off and joined the circus, or stowed away on a pirate ship, or something equally fantastical.

'Ah,' said Miss Frobisher. She gave a small smile. 'Well, what happened was that Mother fell ill. Halfway through the 1921 season. Bronchitis, which was a very serious thing in those days. She was sent back to the country, and it was agreed that Aunt Vanessa – who was in London chaperoning Lizzie – would take care of me as well.

'Now, what Lizzie and I knew, but the adults in my life didn't, was that Aunt Vanessa was a terrible chaperone. She hated late nights, and crowds, and dancing, and everything the season entailed. She would park herself in the corner of the ballroom and be asleep by half past eight. That was when Lizzie and I would escape.'

'Escape?' I leaned forwards. 'Where to?'

'Oh, all sorts of places,' said Miss Frobisher. 'We went to nightclubs. We persuaded our brothers and cousins to sneak us into grown-up parties. And then, after a while, we found ourselves getting invitations in our own right. I was twenty-one by then. I wasn't a débutante any more. That season was the first time I truly understood that I was now an adult, and that if I didn't do something fast, I was going to spend the rest of my life as my parents' unmarried daughter.'

'So what did you do?' I said.

'I got a job,' said Miss Frobisher. 'Writing a Society column for a London newspaper. Miss Sophisticate, I was called. It was an incredibly silly job. I went to parties, and then I wrote down who was there and what they were wearing, who'd designed their dress, and who had gotten engaged to whom.

'The young man who had written the column before me was called James Monroe. He was engaged to a school friend of mine, and he told me about his column – in strictest confidence, of course. He was intending to give it up when he got married and entered his father-in-law's business.

'"Thing is," he told me, topping up my glass. "Thing is, I don't know how the paper is going to replace me. The sort of chap who gets invited to the sort of parties one needs to get invited to doesn't generally want to be sitting up at midnight writing columns on Lady Viola's hat trimming. If you get my drift."'

'I did, and suggested myself immediately for the job. He was initially dubious – "What'll you do when your ma comes back?" – but I waved my hand airily and told him I could "deal" with Mother.'

'I held that job for the rest of the season. I loved it. I loved the secrecy – writing my copy on my uncle's typewriter late at night while the rest of the house was sleeping. I loved the power – saying terrible things about the dress sense of girls who'd snubbed me at parties, laughing at the hairstyles of boys who hadn't asked me to dance. I found some of my columns recently and was so ashamed. I was much too young to have been given a job like that really. I was a very young twenty-one.'

'At the end of that season, I had quite a pile of money hidden in the bottom of a hat box. Mother and Father were leaving London, and both expected me to come back to the country with them. I'd never minded before, but before there had always been Ralph and Sylvia. Now Ralph and Sylvia were married, and there was only me left.

'I knew, with a sinking feeling, that this was what the rest of my life was going to look like. And I knew that it wasn't a life I wanted to live. I also knew that if I wanted to escape my parents' house, I would need some way of earning a living.'

'So what did you do?'

'I went and spoke to my paper's editor and asked him for a full-time job,' Miss Frobisher said. 'He was a bit doubtful at first. He liked my column, but in those days there were very few opportunities for lady journalists. There were the Women's Pages, which meant knitting and cookery and fashion, none of which I knew the first thing about. I had got all the fashion details for my column from Lizzie. You could also be an agony aunt, but they already had one of those. "What else can you write?" he asked me. So I told him I wanted to do investigative work. Undercover operations, that sort of thing. I'd always loved acting and dressing up.

'The editor seemed a bit dubious, but it turned out he had one or two stories that would be easier to investigate with a woman on the staff. He agreed to give me a month's trial.

'As far as I was concerned, that was a done deal. I took a cab back to our London house. Father and Mother were sitting together in the drawing room. "I've got some news!" I told them. "I'm not coming back home. I've got a job. As an investigative journalist. I'm going to investigate iniquity and poverty among the working classes. I'm moving out at the end of the week."

'Pandemonium, of course. There were tears and fury – but actually much less tears and fury than I'd expected. You see, by this point we'd already had Sylvia's pandemonium. I wonder now if my parents had foreseen something of this nature. I think perhaps they were just grateful that I didn't want to go on to the stage or marry the dustman.

'Mother helped me to find a room in a boarding house for unmarried girls. It was a little sparse, but entirely respectable. I had my own room, with a bay window and a washstand with a basin and ewer painted with pictures of laughing milkmaids. Breakfast and dinner provided.

'Society column aside, the newspaper I worked for had a decidedly left-wing bent. I spent a lot of my time writing shock pieces on working conditions in factories, and living conditions in workhouses, hospitals and orphanages. I went on protest marches. I talked to youths in sweatshops. I think my editor had intended to shock me, and possibly to scare me away, by sending me to such places. But I surprised us both by thriving.

'I've always loved talking to people, and I soon discovered how easy it is to make a friend when you're a sympathetic young woman who lends a cigarette or buys a cup of tea. I visited dosshouses and prisons, factories, lunatic asylums and backstreet tenements where families of ten or eleven lived piled up on top of each other in one or two little rooms. It was long, difficult work, often dirty, occasionally dangerous. I was spat at, insulted and threatened. People wrote letters to the newspaper denouncing me as a fake. They didn't believe that my articles could have been written by a woman. But I didn't care. I was young, and I was powerful, and I was probably immortal.

'And because I was the only woman on the investigative staff, I also got the "women's" stories. No knitting patterns. Real stories, about real women. I wrote about the campaign for women's suffrage, and the joy in 1928 when women like myself were given the right to vote. I wrote about women who went to university but weren't allowed to gain degrees, and about the fight for equal pay for women teachers and pensions for women.'

She saw the look on my face and nodded.

'Oh, yes,' she said. 'It's quite a new thing, this idea that a woman should earn the same as a man. A man has to support a family, after all. That's how the argument went.'

'That's awful,' I said.

'It is,' said Miss Frobisher. 'But it's astonishing how hard it was to persuade people of that. And it isn't a battle that has been won yet either. Women still earn less than men, even now, though now it's more subtly done, and harder to fight.

'It was a wonderful thing to be part of, seeing women realise their power and their potential. I covered all sorts of campaigns. Take the fight for pensions for spinsters in the 1930s. I covered their big march through London to Hyde Park, four abreast, all singing:

'"Come spinsters, all attention,
And show that you're alive.
Arise, demand your pension,
When you are fifty-five."

'There was a brass band playing. There were hundreds of women – working women, mostly, waving placards. WE ARE NOT DOWNHEARTED BUT DETERMINED, the banners read. And, A FAIR SHARE FOR ALL. The women sang and waved their banners, and generally looked like they were all off for a nice day at the seaside. It was like a party. And as we marched down the streets, people seemed to feel the same. I'd written articles about protest marches where people had booed or just looked on indifferently, particularly during the Great Depression, where poverty was treated like an embarrassing skin complaint, and people avoided it where possible, in case it was catching.

'On that day, though, no one was looking away and no one was booing. People *cheered*, and waved from the windows of the houses we passed.

'"Good for you!" they called and "Pensions for spinsters!"

'It was wonderfully thrilling.

'When we got to the park, a stage had been set up. When the speakers talked about the work single women did, everyone clapped and waved their banners and agreed that, yes, we were a pretty deserving lot. Afterwards, there were more songs and then the gathering broke up, with all the women who'd come down from the north heading off to visit Buckingham Palace and the Victoria and Albert Museum, and whatever else they thought was necessary on a trip to London.'

'And you won?' I said. 'You did win, didn't you?'

'We did,' said Miss Frobisher. She laughed. 'You'd be astonished at what battles people have won by simply standing up to be counted. Like those young people you see marching in America. They'll win too, mark my words.'

I wasn't so convinced. The young people in America wanted all sorts of things. Free love, and the Bomb banned, mostly. I was in favour of banning the bomb and had a CND button to prove it. I'd sort of assumed it wouldn't happen though. But who knows? I thought of all the battles Miss Frobisher's friends had won – equal pay for women, pensions, university degrees, the vote. It was astonishing when you thought about it.

'It was an exciting time to be a woman,' Miss Frobisher said. 'So many firsts! The first woman to graduate from university. The first woman stockbroker. The first woman MP. A generation of pioneers.'

I felt a little cheated. Miss Frobisher's friends had stolen everything. What did I have left? First woman on the moon?

'When I grow up,' I said, experimentally, 'I'm going to be the first woman on the moon.'

I looked sideways at Miss Frobisher.

'If you like, dear,' she said. 'I always thought it looked like a miserable sort of place, myself.'

So did I, really. I would have liked to go into space if it looked like the space in *Star Wars*, but an airless grey desert wasn't my idea of a good time. Could I be the first woman prime minister? I couldn't even get my brother and sister to do what I told them. So probably not. And anyway, I'd much rather be a protest marcher and get the politicians to ban the Bomb.

Maybe I'd do that. Or maybe I'd be a journalist, like Miss Frobisher. I quite liked the idea of being an investigative journalist. It was the sort of job that impressed people when you told them you did it. Miss Frobisher had impressed me, and even though I didn't know what I wanted to be when I grew up, I was pretty certain I wanted to be impressive.

But Miss Frobisher's thoughts were still with the women marching.

'It's funny really,' she said, 'when you think about it.

If the War hadn't happened, would we still have a set-up like that now? Men having all the choices, and women having none. The War changed everything, you see. Single women weren't an oddity any more. We were an organised collective – or some of us were.'

She leaned forward and poured herself another cup of tea. I watched as she stirred in the milk with her tiny silver teaspoon. She looked small and delicate and utterly unremarkable.

'So is that what you did?' I wasn't sure if the story was over or not. 'Were you an investigating journalist for the rest of your life?'

'Well. Not quite. You see, when I was thirty-nine, the second war broke out. Obviously my paper's priorities changed somewhat then.'

'Did they sack you?' I said.

She laughed. 'Sack me! Certainly not! No, I stayed in London for the first year, covering the Home Front. Then, in 1940, they sent me to Egypt, as a War correspondent. I was there for the rest of the War.'

I boggled. Meek Miss Frobisher? A war correspondent! Wait till I told my brother *that*!

'What was it like?' I said. 'Did they shoot at you?'

'Sometimes.' Miss Frobisher looked pleased to be asked. 'It was... well, parts of it were dreadful. We never got enough sleep, and it was so *hot*, and of course, living in a war zone is its own kind of awful. But even when things were at their hardest, I always had that sense that I was working for something important. Something that meant something. I'd felt the same way in London.

'Sometimes, I'd look at myself and the life I was living, and I'd think, I'm so *lucky*. Here I was, in this strange, beautiful, violent place, bringing back news to all the people waiting at home. To be given the chance to do that ... I was so grateful.'

She paused. I was astonished. *She* was astonishing. I tried to imagine going out to Egypt or somewhere like that and writing about a war, and just not caring about getting married. I knew a few girls who didn't want children, but I didn't know *anybody* who didn't want to be married.

It was getting late. In the street outside, the lamps were coming on one by one. I could smell my mother's shepherd's pie wafting up from downstairs. Pretty soon they'd be calling for me to come down for dinner.

'But didn't you mind, at all?' I said. 'Didn't you miss ... well ...?' I wasn't sure how to put it politely. Kissing? Men?

'You mean sex?' said Miss Frobisher. She threw back her head and laughed delightedly. I could see her small, white teeth in the back of her mouth. 'Ah, my dear,' she said, 'now that's a whole other story.'

I thought about that for a bit.

'Another day?' I said.

'Maybe,' she said. 'When you're older. Go on now, your dinner will be waiting.'

I went, reluctantly.

'I'll be back tomorrow,' I said. 'For piano.'

She nodded.

'Until tomorrow then.'

My mother was dishing up shepherd's pie at the kitchen counter.

'There you are!' she said. 'Can you lay the table for me – quickly now? Kids! Stop fighting! Dinner's ready!'

I went over to the cutlery drawer and began counting out forks.

'You were wrong about Miss Frobisher,' I said.

'Hmm?' said my mother, as my brother and sister came charging in. 'No, don't sit down. Go and wash your hands. Hey! What did I just say? Wash your hands, I said. Now!'

'All those leftover women didn't just do nothing.' I laid the forks out neatly on the table, one for my sister, one for my brother, one for me.

'What?' said my mother. 'No! Go back and do it properly. *Properly*, I said.'

'They didn't just do nothing,' I said. 'All those women. They changed the world.'

But I don't think she heard.

Author Biographies

Theresa Breslin is the Carnegie Medal-winning author of over thirty books for children and young adults, whose work has appeared on stage, radio and television. Her books are read extensively in schools and universities and enjoyed worldwide in many languages. Writings on the First World War include *Remembrance* (now in an updated version with book notes), *Ghost Soldier*, for readers aged 9–12, and a contribution to Michael Morpurgo's anthology *Only Remembered*. 'Shadow and Light' was inspired by Norah Neilson Gray, an artist who, during the First World War, volunteered as a nurse with the Scottish Women's Hospitals organised by Dr Elsie Inglis. The hospital scenes she painted while in France now hang in the Imperial War Museum and Helensburgh Library.

Matt Whyman is the author of several acclaimed novels, including *Boy Kills Man* and *The Savages*. He is married with four children and lives in West Sussex.

Matt says, 'The fog of war often creates difficulties for historians seeking to establish the facts. For storytellers, it can be a liberation, which is what drew me to write about the Gallipoli disaster. The presence of female snipers remains disputed. Many dismiss it outright as a myth, though several compelling accounts from Allied soldiers exist. There is nothing as told through the eyes of such a woman, however, which is what persuaded me to write "Ghost Story". It is said that all fiction contains a grain of truth. At the very least, I hope you find this here in my exploration of what might drive a grieving widow to take aim on the front line.'

Mary Hooper has been writing books for young adults for a while, but some years back she began writing historical fiction and decided she never wanted to write anything else. She does lots of research for whatever period she's writing about, finds tales about things that really happened, then usually invents a central character who has to try and survive all the horrors thrown at them. Sometimes (as in *Newes From The Dead*) the main character is someone who really existed. The idea for 'Storm in a Teashop' came about when Mary was researching *Poppy*, a book about an eighteen-year-old nurse in the First World War, and wondered to herself what sort of people became spies...

Rowena House lived and worked in France as a foreign correspondent for the Reuters news agency. Following further posting to Europe and Africa, she returned to England and started a family. Now settled in Devon, she began writing fiction for her son. Then, in 2012, Bath Spa University offered her a place on their prestigious Masters programme in Writing for Young People. 'The Marshalling of Angélique's Geese' is her winning entry for a short story competition run for the Bath Spa students by Andersen Press. Her initial inspiration was a TV documentary featuring British virologist Professor John Oxford, who is one of the world's leading experts on the 'Spanish' 'flu pandemic.

Melvin Burgess has been writing for young people ever since his first book, *The Cry of the Wolf*, was short-listed for the Carnegie Medal in 1990. Since then he has published over twenty books and won numerous prizes including the Carnegie Medal for *Junk* and the LA Times Book of the Year for *Doing It*. His work has been widely adapted for stage and screen.

Melvin says, 'The idea for "Mother and Mrs Everington" came from a piece by Helen Zenna Smith, from her semi-biographical novel, *Not So Quiet: Stepdaughters of War*. In it, the narrator imagines showing her war-loving mother and her friend around the hospital and shocking them with the terrible injuries she treated every day. I love the voice Helen Zenna Smith uses, which is typical of many women at that time, Suffragettes in particular – so passionate, so militant, so committed to proving their worth. They wanted to show they were men's equal and many saw the War as a chance to do just that. Instead, they found out they were just as fragile.'

Berlie Doherty writes stories, novels, plays and poetry, and has won awards in all fields. She has won the Carnegie Medal twice, for *Granny Was a Buffer Girl* and *Dear Nobody*. Her recent books include *Treason* and *The Company of Ghosts*. Her inspiration for 'Sky Dancer' came from the research she did for *Thin Air*, her play about a First World War pilot, and from Lena Ashwell's invaluable book *Modern Troubadours*, a record of concerts at the Front.

Anne Fine has won the Guardian Children's Book Prize, and both the Carnegie Medal and Whitbread Award twice over. She was the Children's Laureate from 2001–3 and is a Fellow of the Royal Society of Literature. Her books are published in forty-five languages.

Anne says, 'Adults don't have imaginary friends. But if you lost someone precious, imagine what a comfort it would be to think you could still be in touch with them. It's hardly surprising that the parents and widows of so many soldiers were drawn to those who claimed they could talk to the dead.'

Adèle Geras was born in Jerusalem and spent her childhood in many different countries. She was educated at Roedean School, Brighton and St. Hilda's College, Oxford. She has been a writer since 1976 but before that, she was a singer and a French teacher. She lives in Cambridge and has two daughters and three grandchildren.

Adèle says, 'I've written more than ninety books for readers of all ages and what inspired me to write this story was a simple desire to write a spooky love story. The First World War has become a byword for violence and slaughter. But I was not interested in describing the mud and blood of the fields of Flanders, so much as the effect of the War on the girls and women left behind. I set it in Kew Gardens because that's one of my favourite gardens and I wanted the whole story to be full of things we don't associate with war at all: flowers, nice clothes and so on. I also like writing about sisters, maybe because I'm an only child.'

Sally Nicholls was born in Stockton, just after midnight, in a thunderstorm. She has always loved stories, and spent most of her childhood trying to make real life more like an Enid Blyton novel. Her first novel, *Ways to Live Forever*, was published to great acclaim in 2008, and was followed by *Season of Secrets*, *All Fall Down* and *Close Your Pretty Eyes*. She has won many awards, including the Waterstone's Children's Book Prize and the Glen Dimplex New Writer of the Year Award. Sally is fascinated by the generation of 'spare women', who challenged so many 1920s assumptions, and opened the doors to so many opportunities that we now take for granted. Miss Frobisher's story in 'Going Spare' is fictional, but her account of a ball filled almost entirely with women is taken from a real description from that period.

LOSING IT

edited by
Keith Gray

Will you, won't you? Should you, shouldn't you?

Have you . . .?

A gift? Or a burden?

MELVIN BURGESS, ANNE FINE, KEITH GRAY, MARY
HOOPER, SOPHIE MCKENZIE, PATRICK NESS, BALI RAI
AND JENNY VALENTINE.

Losing It is an original and thought-provoking
collection of stories from some of today's leading
writers for young people: some
funny, some moving, some
haunting but all revolving
around the same subject –
having sex for the first time.

Everything you ever wanted to
know about virginity but your
parents were too embarrassed
to tell you.

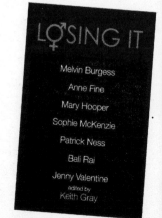

LOSING IT

Melvin Burgess

Anne Fine

Mary Hooper

Sophie McKenzie

Patrick Ness

Bali Rai

Jenny Valentine
edited by
Keith Gray

9781849390996 £5.99

NEXT

edited by
Keith Gray

A collection of short stories about the afterlife by some of today's leading writers for teens: Keith Gray, Jonathan Stroud, Philip Ardagh, Frank Cottrell Boyce, Malorie Blackman, Sally Nicholls, Julie Bertagna and Gillian Philip.

Heaven? Hell? Purgatory? Reincarnation? Ghosts? Buried? Nothing . . .?

What happens after you die?

Will you go out with a bang? Or find a peace that only you can see?

Is heaven spending eternity reliving your happiest memories? Or is your future in someone else's thoughts?

Could it even be that you leave a part of yourself behind?

'This excellent collection provokes, reassures and above all surprises' *Books for Keeps*

'I thought "this is the best one" for each and every story' *Bookwitch*

9781849393003 £6.99

HAUNTED

A FANTASTIC COLLECTION OF GHOST STORIES FROM TODAY'S LEADING CHILDREN'S AUTHORS

'A chilling slice of horror. An excellent balance of traditional and modern and a perfect pocket-money purchase for winter evenings.' *Daily Mail*

Derek Landy, Philip Reeve, Joseph Delaney, Susan Cooper, Eleanor Updale, Jamila Gavin, Mal Peet, Matt Haig, Berlie Doherty, Robin Jarvis and Sam Llewellyn have come together to bring you eleven ghost stories: from a ghost walk around York; to a drowned boy, who's determined to find someone to play with; to a lost child trapped in a mirror, ready to pull you in; to devilish creatures, waiting with bated breath for their next young victim; to an ancient woodland reawakened. Some will make you scream, some will make you shiver, but all will haunt you gently long after you've put the book down.

9781849393218 £6.99

THE DRAGON BOOK

EDITED BY JACK DANN AND GARDNER DOZOIS

Fearful fire-breathing creatures of great savagery and greed or noble creatures mystically bonded to the warriors who ride them? In *The Dragon Book* today's greatest fantasy writers reignite the flame with legendary tales that will consume the imagination.

These stories make up an incredible collection that will challenge perceptions of dragons – and leave you watching the skies . . .

Contributors include Garth Nix, Jonathon Stroud, Tad Williams, Tamora Pierce, Diana Wynne Jones, Cecelia Holland, and Tanith Lee.

9781849391009 £7.99

Burning Issy

MELVIN BURGESS

'Are you frightened of dying, Issy?'

Issy doesn't know where she came from or who she is.
Night after night, she has the same nightmare: she
burns in a fire and at the heart of the flames is a face
she dare not look at. Fear and superstition are
everywhere. She must run – from the Witch-finder,
from the evil hag who wants her, from those she loves
and maybe even from her own true nature...

'Vivid and atmospheric ...
Unforgettable stuff'
Guardian

'Brutally honest ... this
remarkable historical novel
erupts into life from the very
first page.'
Financial Times

9781849393973 £5.99

Treason

BERLIE DOHERTY

Who matters most? Your father or your king?

Will Montague is a page to Prince Edward, son of
King Henry VIII. As the King's favourite, Will gains
many enemies in Court. His enemies convince the
King that Will's father has committed treason and he
is thrown into Newgate Prison. Will flees Hampton
Court and goes into hiding in the back streets of
London. Lost and in mortal danger, he is rescued by
a poor boy, Nick Drew. Together they must brave
imprisonment and death as they embark on a great
adventure to set Will's father free.

'Doherty paints a very vivid
picture . . . almost Shardlake
for young readers.'
Independent on Sunday

'A beautifully paced and measured
story. 5 stars.'
Books for Keeps

9781849391214 £6.99